THE GREAT ADVENTURES
OF A COMMON WALKING
TREE

WOODBEE ISLAND TALES

THE GREAT ADVENTURES OF A COMMON WALKING TREE

BOOK 1

By John O. Evans
Illustrated By Cynthia D. Jackson

This is a work of fiction.
Names, places, characters, and incidents
are the product of the author's imagination.
Any resemblance to any actual persons, living
or dead, organizations, or events is entirely
coincidental. There are, of course, allusions
to our Creator's Words.

Paperback: 9798391407935
First paperback edition July 2023.
Cover images and illustrations by
Cynthia D. Jackson
Photographs, as well as published, by
John O. Evans

Acknowledgements

I thank Cynthia D. Jackson very much
for the wonderful cover art and the great
illustrations throughout the book.

I also thank those who have encouraged
and supported me. I thank James Hunt for his
encouragement and helpful suggestions. Besides
being the great illustrator for this book, Cynthia D.
Jackson also encouraged me and provided very
frequent suggestions when asked. I thank Cynthia.
And I thank my wife, Soon Geum Song: "Thank you
for the encouragement and support which you
provided through this walking tree's
adventure."

TABLE OF CONTENTS

1

A WALKING TREE

It should come as no surprise, of course, that this seed-through-tree story was written from a tree's point of view. For only a tree would know certain things of a tree's life. Also, for obvious reasons, a tree could never tell a story from any other point of view, even if a tree ever wished to. In addition, not only is any tree story quite easy to read, but it's also, of course, the most fruitful. And so this is a tree story as told by a tree.

Now if by some miracle our Planter has made any nontrees with the ability to read, I'm sure that He's also given them at least a bit of tree sense, certainly enough sense to understand a tree story such as this. We will now leave the early sprouting of this tree tale by mentioning those two proverbs popular among well-read trees: "Every good tale begins with a seed;" and "Home's the place you'd never leave, even if you ever could."

In my beginning, there was utter darkness, as far back as I can remember. And there was such silence, for some time, and this before I had even learned of time. But then I found my-seed-self stretching and stretching, with all these noisy crackling sounds all around me. No! I was wrong! The sounds were me! I, who-seed-ever I was, was being pulled both downward and upward at the same time, nearly pulled apart, and this before even finding out who I was! In hindsight, I know now that while the darkness of the earth was pulling at my roots, the bright light above was pulling at my growing crown. "What will become of me, whoever me is?" This was my first real seed thought.

But suddenly, there were these huge snappings, cracklings, poppings, rumblings and thunderings! And the whole blue sky was suddenly bursting apart in every direction while falling at the same time, falling down on me! Or was I flying upward?! I didn't yet know. Now the bright, empty sky was less empty, being all around me, as well as up above!

I suddenly noticed that this bright light was not only everywhere about me, but it was me! Or was it in me?! It was changing me, making its home within my broken shell. Who was I? I still didn't know, and I still didn't know whether I should know. Oh, my seedling days were so confusing! But then I did finally ask my-seedling-self, "Who is me?" And, yes, this was my first real seedling thought! I was now a seedling, who-seedling-ever I was!

Every-tree in the neighborhood was now coming into view. "How strange!" And then my whole, new bright world began to shrink and to shrink, smaller and smaller, as suddenly as it had all appeared, the new earth below becoming more and more distant, farther and farther away from a growing sapling's view. My huge neighbors (I later learned who they were.) were becoming a little less and less like the gigantic giants they had been at first. I was climbing higher and higher toward that distant blue sky. And yet... at the same time, I somehow knew that I was also drilling deep down into the dark earth. I couldn't see it, but I could sense it. And saplings, as you know, have very good senses.

Yes, I had the usual growing pains. But that was okay for a growing sapling! For I just kept reaching upward, towering farther above the fading earth, or so was my tiny sapling thought. I was aiming higher and higher for a blue sky of light. My first real sapling thought? "I'm home!"

When did I first notice that I was very different from my neighbors? It was sometime later that I began to compare my plain, simple tree-self to my lofty, fully leaf-crowned neighbors. I could have been one of their tiny thin sticks stuck in the mud! I held onto my poor, flattened crown, while all my neighborly giants each wore their proud, full-leafed crowns way up high in the sky.

Poor sapling-me... I had such a hard time growing up there. I soon learned that it was these giant crowns of my neighborhood that were frightening away the life-giving light I so longed for. How did I like home, where I was standing daily in the great dark shadows of giants? Of course, I learned this valued proverb early in life: "Home's the place you'd never leave, even if you ever could."

Though this was home, some trees began whispering among them-tree-selves, "He's too different..." Let me explain how different I became besides having this simple flat crown and thin trunk. You see, while their roots were mostly in the darkness of the earth, as they should be of course, many of mine were reaching downward from much further above the earth. Most of their roots were hidden, but most of mine were in full view. We all guessed that they had many roots hidden under the earth. We have all seen some unfortunate neighbor fall over for some reason, perhaps because of a storm, leaving all their roots high up in the air to dry. "Roots were meant to be hidden," they often reminded me. But what could I do? I didn't want to be different... And so, yes, being so different was embarrassing.

Unfortunately, a poor, old neighbor did fall over sometime later, falling over right on top of me! I guess he had lost his grip in the dark earth and just toppled over, knocking me over with him. But while he was sadly a lost soon-to-dry tree now, having no hope for survival, I suddenly found my-tree-self just picking up my roots and walking away from my birthplace, away from home!

Oh! Every-tree was in such shock, including me! You see, my roots started extending further out from my trunk, pulled me out from under that poor, old neighbor, and then lifted me right up, facing the sky again! Here I was now, standing some distance from my home! I had just walked away from where I was trapped! How happy I was!

But, no, not my neighbors! They had even more questions about me after that. I could hear them whispering even more among them-tree-selves. What were they saying? Did I hear, "ghost"? Did they think I was a ghost? I think they did. But I wasn't! I was still a living tree! It's just that now I could walk! I was a walking tree!

I began to hear other whisperings among neighbors at that time. I heard something like, "I hear they dropped him off at night," and "There were two of them, I hear." What could this gossip mean? Were they talking about me?

I thought they were, and so I asked our forest giant who stood next to me, "Grandaddy, how did I get here?"

"Grandson, now I can tell you how you got here. Every-tree knows that two of some kind left you here among us at night. Of what kind they were, no-tree knows. For no-tree knows who saw those two. And so where they came from and where they went, no-tree here knows this either.

Grandson, this is your home, and 'Home's the place you'd never leave, even if you ever could.' Grandson, you have been with us since you were just a tiny seed. We are your family."

"Yes, Grandaddy. Thank you, Grandaddy."

I knew that Grandad told me all that he knew. This was home.

Now soon after that, I saw my first wonder of the skies. I shouted, "Look, Grandaddy! Clouds of flowers!" They were right up there above us! There were bright and colorful clouds of flying flowers way up high in the sky!

"Oh, my grandson, learn these words: 'First seeing clouds of flowers flying about is welcoming a season beginning to sprout.'"

"Oh, Grandaddy, what does that mean?"

"Grandson, your season of new beginnings is sprouting! Welcome it!"

"Yes, Grandaddy!"

But then something began happening to me, and nothing after that was the same. As if my differences weren't bad enough, I also began to have strange dreams at night. I soon tried to keep them to my-tree-self the best I could, but I am not very good at that. Here are the talks about my dreams:

"Why are you looking so downcast, Grandson?"

"I had a dream, Grandaddy."

"Tell me."

"Well... I was up on the heights, up above our forest, and there were three of me. I could see me-three clearly - one, two, three. And then there were walking grass seeds walking up to me-three, planting themselves into the earth. They grew up tall and waved 'Good-bye'. Last, we-three came down from the heights, happily walking home. What do you think, Grandaddy?"

"No tree has foolish dreams like this! On the heights?! How will you become taller than me, Grandaddy of trees? Walking grass seeds and walking trees? Seeds and trees don't walk! Your branches aren't much taller than your roots, Grandson. Hmmmfff!"

I then decided not to have any more dreams. But still, there was another one.

"Why this dead-wood look, Grandson?"

"Well, it's not important, really..."

"Another dream? Tell me."

"Well... this time I was walking with many of me. They, or me, were all around me. First, we all had much fruit. But next, I was trying to pull my-tree-self away from many of me, while they were disappearing into thin gray earth-crawlers! I finally pulled free and walked up toward the heights."

"Weren't the three of you enough in your first dream? Now, you must have many of you? What kind of dream is this, Grandson? Trees disappearing into earth-crawlers? Never happens! And again, you're walking the heights above your grandaddy? No more of these dreams!"

"Yes, Grandaddy..."

But yes, there was a third one.

"Why looking down? Another dream? Tell it to me, Grandson."

"Well... Oh..."

"Yes...?"

"Well... I was walking through many clearings and forests. Then I saw some trees with no faces! And some trees walked straight, while others walked in circles! Grandaddy, I don't understand why I have these dreams. What could this one mean, Grandaddy?"

"What a crazy dream! Mean?! It means nothing! Treeberish! Nothing but silly treeberish! Clearings and forests?! What's a clearing?! Trees walking again? Trees don't walk! I knew when I saw you rising up as a seedling that you were too different!"

"But Grandaddy! You asked me to tell you!"

A little later, the whisperings among my neighbors became like echoing thunder. Somehow, my dreams had become common knowledge, and no-tree, of course, liked what they heard of my lofty dreams. After all, what tree would like a tiny tree walking on the heights over their crown? Grandad could stand the noisy rumblings no longer.

So Grandad finally burst, "What trouble your dreams have brought us, Grandson! All this thundering and rumbling! If you could truly walk away from here as you claim by your foolish dreams, I would tell you, 'Walk up above your neighbors! Walk high above Grandaddy! Walk on the heights! Grandson, go then!'"

Now, all the neighbors were suddenly quiet while Grandad was thundering. And there was still some silence after his thundering stopped.

And then it happened. I was walking. I was walking away... My forward roots reached out toward the great light before me as rear roots began drying and getting dragged behind me. My forward roots were now taking me away from home. And I couldn't stop them, or maybe I could... I don't really know. All I knew for sure was that I was walking. I told my-tree-self, "I'm walking home!"

"What?!" was all Grandad could say at first when I was walking past him with a growing smile.

Leaving our forest wasn't the problem. Every-tree already recognized that I was no longer a young sapling. I was now a grownup tree. Lately, they would even look my way and say, "Look! The tree!" The problem was that I was leaving. No-tree ever just got up and left. They always remained at home where they had sprouted and grown. You see, trees don't walk. But now, they were watching me, a walking tree, just walking away. And as they watched, their faces became longer and longer...

"Farewell, Grandad! Farewell, neighbors! Farewell to all!"

But as I walked along through the forest saying my good-byes, I soon stopped, turned, and shouted, "I'm walking home! But I may return for a visit!"

I had walked some distance when I heard the rumbling of a thunderous voice say, "Return for a visit!!!"

"Grandad, yeah!!!" I shouted from the top of my branches.

The thunder rumbled once more, "After walking home!!!"

2

SEVEN ORCHARDS

I walked onward for days, mentioning to strange
trees along the way of that great light which I
followed, the light before me. And many strange
trees listened to me with delight.

Now, I could finally tell I was leaving our
forest behind. The light was shining upon me. And

now, I really knew what a clearing was. It was right there before me. And just like my dreams, there was me, many of me, or so I thought. But, no, they weren't me at all.

They only looked like me. They were tall and slender. They had the same lowly, flattened crown that I have, and the same walking roots all spread about them. And they were walking, just like me! They were my kind! I was not different here! We trees were the same kind of tree, walking trees!

But then, something was unexpected about these trees that looked like me. They all walked in one straight line, all together at the same time, one after the other, no tree walking out of line. "How strange!" I thought. "Is this how I have to walk? Must I walk like an ant in an ant line, all following the leader, following the tree walking before me?"

They tirelessly walked in their line, and when the tree leader reached the clearing's end, he turned around and led his tree line right back again, back to where they had started. I got in line with them, joining them in the back. And we trees were walking along just fine.

But then some questioned me about my-tree-self, "Walk as we do, walking truth. By the way, who are you?"

"Well, I don't know what you want to call me-tree, but some in my forest call me 'Grandson'. And I'm doing my best to walk like you, trying to fit in with you trees."

"'You-trees,' we trees are not. We are Truth-trees of Truth Orchard. Follow, fellow Truth-tree, and we trees will walk together in truth, just as our lead-tree walks. He has been tested and found to be true."

And walk we did. We walked all day, up and back, and up and back again, in that clearing, walking in a straight line of truth.

How wonderfully they all walked! It is not an easy thing to walk all day in a straight line of truth. But they did it without complaint and without growing tired. They all kept at their hard work all the day long.

But what of love? It was great to see them daily walking truth, being careful not to follow an evil leader, but I could not see love among them.

This may sound strange to some trees, but I did know something of love in my first home, where I grew from seed through sapling-hood to grownup tree. For example, one day some strange creature climbed up Grandad. And it was hungry! Oh, how I feared for Grandad! "Grandaddy, what is that thing climbing you?!"

"It is a tree-climber, Grandson. It climbs us trees, disappearing leaves and sometimes branches."

This tree-climber had a long round trunk lying on its side with four roots used for walking and climbing. It also had a long, pointed face with two long leaves and two twisted, leafless branches, all growing upward from its crown. It had long thin roots hanging below its face and below its trunk. And one root with smaller roots was sticking out from its end. (I was told later that some call it a "goat".)

I shouted, "Grandaddy! I fear for you!"

"Oh, don't worry about me. I'm fine. I'm a giant tree. They only tickle me a little. But you, Grandson, I fear for you. You're very small. If they notice you, that could be your end. Grandson, let's remain quiet, and they'll soon leave. Don't fear for me."

I knew something of love among my neighbors, but I could not find it among Truth-trees. I'll tell you what happened one day, which made this very clear.

As our daily practice was, we were walking our single line, with me walking near the back. But suddenly, I couldn't move. I couldn't take another step.

"What is it? What's happened?" I thought.

Truth-trees were not kind: "Move along! Keep in step! Walk this line of truth!"

"I can't! Something stopped me! Please look! What is it?" But I did not get help from any-tree. They just kept walking around me, walking along their way of truth. I called out, "Stop! Help!" But they kept walking onward, leaving me behind.

I looked about and finally found the problem. It was a terrible, hungry nontree thing! I had never seen such a thing before! It had a round, fat trunk, its trunk lying on its side like other nontree creatures. But just along the top of its sideways trunk it had the strangest thick row of roots, sticking straight up! What an odd sight it was! Also, near the bottom of its face it had a wide, white stripe circling its hungry opening. And it had two sharp, yellow branches coming straight up from the bottom of that opening! It also had a thick ring of white about its trunk, along with the usual four roots used for walking and running. Finally, this creature had the usual thin root at its rear. What I noticed most was that its hungry opening was quickly disappearing my precious roots!

I again called out, "Help! Save me from this hungry thing! Help!" But no-tree even lifted a branch to help me. Oh, how lonely and afraid I felt among those loveless Truth-trees.

"It's disappearing my roots! When they're gone, I'll fall down, and it'll disappear all of me!" I shouted to my-tree-self. "What can I do? Is there no-tree to help me!" What could I do? Without a thought, I looked up to the sky and shouted, "Can anyone help me? Hello! Please help!"

"Reeeiii!!! No one can help you! You must die!" shouted this hungry thing at my roots, while looking straight at me. Then it went back to disappearing me, starting with my roots.

I jumped when I heard this thing speak, but I quickly shouted back, "But why?! Why must I die?!"

I got no answer, for at that moment, two other hungry-runners went racing past both of us with a "Reeeiii!!!", the lone hungry one pausing its root munching just long enough to look up at these two scurrying past.

At the next moment, I saw it! My help! It was a huge tree crown falling from the sky! Only this tree crown had no trunk! Oh, yes, it was a crown-flyer like the little ones I often see, but this one was so much bigger! It was a giant crown-flyer! It had the crown of two large upper branches full of leaves, one on this side and one on the other. And, yes, it had those two roots below, pointing downward toward the earth (toward the hungry-runner disappearing me at this time), with the four sharp roots at the ends of both hanging roots.

Though much like smaller crown-flyers, this one had to be their king, with its huge black crown! And, oh, how it stood out! Its face was white except for those two black and yellow knots near the top and that hooked, yellow disappearing branch at the center! It must have been hungry, but it looked so angry, that King-flyer!

The King-flyer was dropping like a big rock from the sky, aiming right for that hungry beast! That beast had already gone back to busily disappearing my roots, when suddenly, King-flyer hit that hungry beast with a great "Thud!" greatly shaking us both, while the beast let out a deafening scream, its disappearing opening opened wide with all white and yellow branches out in the light! For King-flyer's pair of four piercing roots, while opened wide, firmly stabbed that beast into its sides, while at once lifting it up, the flyer now flying toward his waiting sky, carrying away that screaming hungry-runner, which was now tightly grasped in Sky-king's roots!

As I was looking upward at the two disappearing into the sky, Sky-king turned toward me, shouting, "Eeeyichaaa! Thank your Maker!"

"Yes!" was all I had time to say, with the two quickly disappearing into the sky! But while looking up, I shouted up toward beyond the sky, "I thank you, our Maker, You who watch over me-tree! Thank you!!!"

I spied a little crown-flyer nearby. I called to it, "You! Little crown-flyer! Can you help me-tree?!"

It answered, "Chirp! You know, we sky-rangers don't talk to many of your kind. But our Maker told me to stay near you and to grant your request. What is your request, walking earth-watcher?"

"Please, follow those two hungry-runners which ran past me-tree! See where they go and what is spoken there! Please!"

"Chirp! I'll do as you ask!"

And with that, the little crown-flyer was gone, flying after those two hungry-runners!

Now some time later, that little crown-flyer
returned. And she gave me a very detailed report,
for crown-flyers make very good spies. They
observe and remember everything! I asked her to
give me the complete report with all the strange
words, which she cheerfully did. The observant
reader will find the little crown-flyer's report below.
I now ask my tree readers to read it patiently; for it
is difficult to understand, being in the little spy's
own crown-flyer words.

"Chirp! I followed those two peccaries, and
they led me to the dark castle of the wicked
Stanamon. They entered the gates and reported to
their master, Swibeast. Swibeast is one of those
animal-human beasts. The head was swine, and the
body was man. Such an ugly thing! Following are
my observations and the conversations I heard in
the castle:

"Is that troublesome walking tree in your
bellies now?"

"Reeeiii!!! No, Master!!! The eagle came
down from the sky! It attacked us three and carried

one away! Only we two live! We quickly ran here to report to Master!!!"

"Very well, little peccaries. You must be hungry... Go report to the kitchen as helpers before the meal."

"Reeeiii!!! Yes, Master!!!"

The two hurried off toward the kitchen with one saying to the other, "Reeeiii! Do you know how to cook? I don't."

Swibeast then entered the castle, and I found an open window at Stanamon's throne room. I secretly perched there. Everything Stanamon wore was black: pointed hat, vest, pants, and boots. But his ugly, twisted face was gray and difficult to look at. Stanamon was standing near a pool of water before his throne. Swibeast entered the throne room, stopped and waited.

The water then burst into purple flames with a thunderous voice shouting from below, "Why's that walking tree still walking?! He's troubling my kingdom with talk of light! Darken it, Stanamon!!!"

"Yes, Lord Serpothel! It will be done!!!"

A red flame burst up toward the high stone ceiling, bits of stone falling to the floor below.

"Swibeast, you failed!"

"Reeeiii!!! King Stanamon!!!"

Swibeast fell to the floor before his master.

"Stand up, you fool! You will not fail again."

Stanamon turned toward Snabeast, "Have Crobeast come here at once!"

"Ssss!!! Yesss, King!!!"

Swibeast and Crobeast stood before their king.

Stanamon said, "Crobeast, have your crow spies find the location and direction of this walking tree which speaks of light. Report to Swibeast here!"

"CAA!!! Yes, King!!!"

"Swibeast, send your peccaries again! This time, make sure that walking tree of light stops its talking!!!"

"Reeeiii!!! Yes, King!!!"

"Now, you two come near for a snack."

The three were eating and drinking, the two beasts making sounds of pleasure.

"Reeeiii! Yum! Delicious!"

"CAA! Yum! Yum!"

"You beasts like this snack? Hogchef!!! Tell these beasts what we eat and drink!"

"Gre... Gre... Gggreeeiii!!! Yes, King!!! Today, you're drinking walking-tree wine. This is pig and peccary blood sausage, mostly pig. And that's crow cake!"

"Hmmm..." mumbled two beasts.

"Very good, Hogchef! Go now!"

Stanamon now turned toward the beasts: "Go! End that walking tree! You beasts of pig and crow bloods, go now!!!"

When I turned to fly away, I was noticed by a crow. So I swiftly flew into a nearby earth-watcher and perched on its far side. Just then a flock of crows raced past me.

This is my report! May our Maker help Earth-watcher! Chirp!"

"Walking-tree wine? I don't know what that is, but it doesn't sound good!"

"Chirp! It's not!"

"What's a peccary, and what's a crow?"

"Chirp! You call the peccary a hungry-runner, and the crow is a sky-ranger like me. But it's bigger, and it's black."

"I see... They're disappearing their own, peccaries and crows?! I must warn them!"

"Chirp! Try if you must, but they'll never listen to you!"

"Oh? They won't? Well, another thing... You said Swibeast was an animal and human something?"

"Chirp! Yes! An animal-human beast. Let's see... How do I explain this? Well, animals have four legs and humans have two."

"I see... What's a 'leg'?"

"Chirp! Hmmm... Look! I have two legs."

Sky-ranger than did a little dance. First, she danced a bit toward one end of the tree's branch and then toward the other end. It was a very nice little dance indeed. You see, we trees know something about dancing, too.

"Oh! You mean the two roots you stand and dance on?"

"Chirp! Yes! Well, animals have four legs for walking and running, and humans have two. But a beast like Swibeast is not an animal or a human! No!!! It's an ugly something different! Its head comes from an animal like a peccary, and its body comes from a human like... maybe a Stanamon."

"Oh, okay... Now what's 'head' and 'body'?"

"Chirp! That's easy! See my head? I turn it this way and that. And with it I see you and I hear you and I say to you, 'Chirp! Chirp!'"

"Oh! Really? Well, do I have a head, too?"

"Well, most heads are up high on top of the body. But you have all your green leaves up there! But, yes, I think you have a head! It's down here below your green leaves, right there from where you see me and from where you speak to me! So yes! That's your head! It has your face on it! I'm sure!"

"Wow! I have a head, too! Okay... So it's below my green crown... Hmmm... almost half-way up my trunk... from where I ask my questions. This... This is my head?" I blinked my seeing knots some.

"Chirp! Yes! I think so!"

"And body? Do I have a body?"

"Well, you did call it your trunk. And about half way up your trunk is... is your head. But, no, I don't think you have a body, Earth-watcher! Let's call that your trunk! But one day you might see an animal head on a human body! And, well, that is a very strange, ugly thing indeed!

Look! About 'body'. My head is on my body! And these on my body are my wings. I fly with them. So, of course, I have a sky-ranger head on a sky-ranger body! That's my beauty! But you too, Earth-watcher! You have your own beauty from our Maker. Your beauty is your trunk that stands between crown and roots, and... and your friendly face right there, with its special palm tree mark, smiling at me from the middle of your trunk! Both you and I have our beauty from our Maker! But not the beasts! No! Our Maker didn't make them! Ugly things they are! Ugly things!"

"I have a palm tree mark on my face? What's a palm tree?"

"Oh, you're funny! You're a palm tree!"

"Me-tree? But what could this mark on my face mean?"

"I don't know. That's probably more than I could ever think about... But I know it's a special mark!"

"Wow! Some trees said it looked funny! But I never knew it was special! Me-tree, a palm tree? So... little friend, if our Maker didn't make those ugly beasts, then who did?"

"My guess is that something evil like Stanamon made something ugly like that! Not our Maker! No!"

"Oh, I see... They do sound ugly! I think that if we trees were smart enough to make something ugly like a beast, well, I think we never would! I think we trees are too smart for that!"

"Chirp! And I think we sky-rangers must be too smart to do something foolish like that, too! Thank our Maker!"

"Yes, thank our Maker! And thank you, little crown-flyer! Your report helps a lot! Now I know who the hungry-runners serve. That evil, gray Stanamon and that Serpothel of purple fire! Oh!

And you call the hungry-runners 'peccaries'! And
they work with Stanamon's crows! And the ugly
beasts have animal heads and human bodies! Ha!
I've learned a lot today! Oh, and I almost forgot!
I've got my own head, speaking from right here,
half-way up my trunk! Right?!"

"Chirp! Yes, that's right!"

"Thank you again! May our Planter help
you! Farewell, little crown-flyer!"

"Chirp! Farewell!"

And off she flew.

"So me, a tree, has a head, too? How funny!
Ha! What tree would have known?! But I wonder
who can tell me why my crown is up so high above
my seeing and speaking head? Oh well... I'll just
have to keep that question on my crown for another
time."

Now after losing roots to the hungry-runner
while Truth-trees just walked around me, I knew
for certain that little love lived among them. But I
also learned that there's One who lives beyond the
sky. And He loves me and listens to my cries. He

sends me help. Now, I know to daily thank Him, our Maker.

Because I never knew love among the Loveless-trees (That's what I call them.), I was so hoping to move along. And as it turned out, very soon after the Sky-king rescue, my roots pulled at me. They were pulling me away again.

"Onward again," I thought. "Onward on the path of my dreams."

Loveless Orchard began to shout at me: "Hey! Wrong way! What are you doing, Truth-tree?! Come back! We don't go that way! We don't walk among the likes of them! They don't walk in truth, and they can't even walk!"

But very soon their shouts changed: "Hey! Never come back then! Go on! You're no Truth-tree!" But I did notice that a few of them were holding their words to themselves.

My roots were pulling me onward toward my dreams, and I could only listen to their shouts behind me. Occasionally, I called out a farewell. But I heard none in return, the truth line of Loveless-trees left far behind.

Surprisingly for a light-loving tree such as me, I was now walking deeper and deeper into another dark forest of strange trees. Again, there were no walking trees to be seen. This is how my conversations with strange trees went.

"Who are you, Tree? How can you walk?"

"You can call me Me-tree, and I walk because I walk."

But the thought suddenly came to me, and so I told the strange trees this: "I walk because our Planter, the Maker of the sky and the earth, made me-tree, and others like me-tree, to walk. I'm walking toward the light on the heights. Remember your Planter while young, Strange-trees! Remember Him while you still stand tall! Farewell!"

"Farewell, Me-tree!"

And I was soon leaving this dark forest of welcoming strange trees, coming into another clearing. Here was an orchard, another orchard of my dreams.

This one was very much unlike the first. I came out into the light of this clearing, and I saw them, many more trees like me, walking trees. But how different these trees were from Loveless-trees!

Though these trees looked storm-torn and poor as they walked along, they produced a lot of fruit! I then remembered that I hadn't seen much fruit while walking among Loveless-trees.

Now not only did these trees bear much fruit, they were also rich in love. They shared their fruit with any who hungered. They said their fruit was both a gift from our Planter and an offering to Him.

I thought, "They know Him! They speak of Him! Yes! These are my kind of walking trees! This must be home!!!"

But there were some problems spoken of here, a present one and a greater future one. A seer told these trees, "Our Maker knows the evil words spoken against us by that forest which calls itself 'Maker's Orchard'. Be comforted, Rich-trees. He knows them by another name, 'Serp Forest'. They are not His."

Also, other Rich-tree seers spoke of strange woodsmen, who would come to Rich Orchard, bringing their axes of pain and death. What was a woodsman? All I knew then was that they walked on two roots. And the reader's guess is as good as mine was as to what an axe is. (Only later did I find out.) But we knew that it would bring much trouble to Rich-trees, even bringing death to some. The seers comforted Rich-trees, saying that our Planter loves them and watches over them.

"We can't always understand our Planter's ways," I thought to my-tree-self.

Oh, how I loved it there! Though they were very poor (They called themselves "Poor Orchard".), oh, how rich in fruit and love they were! I would have stayed there in a shake of a branch if I could have, even with that future woodsmen threat.

But our Planter had other plans for me. I hadn't yet walked my dreams. And so my Planter was now turning me round about toward His great light. I was walking outward and onward again!

"Farewell, Rich-trees! Planter is taking me away again for walking my dreams! Remember our Maker! He watches over you!"

"Farewell, Brother-tree! Walk your dreams! Go with our Planter! Farewell!"

And so I was again on my way. I walked through another dark forest, which by the way, the Rich-trees never tried to turn me away from. And I had more of the same talks along the way, speaking of our Planter and of their need to remember Him while young and to thank Him. I walked along my way and came to the third orchard, which was very unlike the first two.

There they were, walking trees like me, walking about in the light of their clearing. These trees had something very good about them. Many were true to our Maker. I heard that they even remained faithful to our Maker when one of their own was destroyed because of love for Him.

But some of the trees here walked in darkness, following evil. They followed an ancient teaching, which taught them to mindlessly walk about while bumping into other trees and to offer sacrifices up to the lord of darkness, to Serpothel!

Oh, those trees of the darkness looked so strange! They were no longer the usual brown and green! They had trunks of gray and crowns of red! But not only that, they even hopped everywhere they went! What a strange sight! They hopped about like the little green hoppers of the ponds! I wondered, "Are these even trees anymore?"

I call this forest Castle Orchard. A castle is a hollow hill of stone, in which things dwell, sometimes such evil things! The evil Castle-trees hopped around a large, dark castle there, which was central to their orchard!

I will now tell of another attack by hungry-runners that hit me like lightning, this one being near the end of my Castle Orchard visit. I saw them turn my way before they hit. There were three this time, and all three were aiming right for me!

"How can Sky-king help me this time?! There are too many!!!" I shouted to my-tree-self. But again, up toward the sky, I hollered, "There are three! Oh, You who stand beyond the skies! Help me-tree, please!!!" The three hit me all at once with the great force of their hunger. "Oh, help me!"

They were all at my forward roots, so I quickly swung around, trying to move them to my other ones. "I need my walking roots!" Two of them were now disappearing my back roots. I shouted to the hungry one at my front roots, "Oh, hungry-runner! Why disappear me-tree?! Swibeast and Stanamon disappear peccaries for snacks! Run and save your-peccary-self!!!"

It snorted, "Reeeiii!" while disappearing my walking roots. "You lie, walking tree!" it grunted. "And you will die!"

"I tell the truth!"

Sky-king was nowhere to be seen, but… there! Another nontree was approaching! "What's this?!" It was slowly moving toward the hungry-runners, now crouching low, looking them over… "Are you my help?! But when?!"

It suddenly sprang forward and put its sharp hunger branches, many of them, into that hungry-runner at my front roots. There was loud squealing with such a struggle! This orange-spotted runner was sinking its white disappearing branches deep into the beast's trunk!

How wonderful! The hungry thing stopped disappearing my forward roots! I now had a chance to escape! The shocked hungry-runner was now quickly disappearing into that orange-spotted creature, as its two friends just suddenly disappeared on their own, running away in a hurry!

I was hobbling a bit now, but no bother. What mattered most was that I was free of those hungry-runners. "Oh, thank you our Planter!"

What was this orange-spotted creature? I had not seen one before this, nor had I ever heard of one. I will describe it. Like other runners of the forest, it had that long, round trunk, which lay on its side, with the four roots for running. But it was bigger than most. It was the size of seven hungry-runners! It's bark? White with many orange spots, each circled by black. Also unlike other runners, it had many long, thin, white roots sticking out from that central black knot on its face, half pointing out this side and half the other. This orange-spotted runner had the usual sharp, white branches pointing downward in its disappearing opening, but they were much bigger, much sharper, than those of other runners! How frightening these branches must be to a hungry-runner! Of course, it had the one thin root sticking out the back. I learned that day that the King-flyer (or Sky-king) wasn't the only one the hungry-runners feared. I hear some call this orange-spotted runner a "jaguar".

I soon said my farewells to those Castle-trees who were true to our Planter, and they, in turn, sent their "farewells" to me. I was again happily walking on my way into another dark forest of strange trees, looking forward to the next clearing. Would the next orchard be another Rich Orchard? "Won't it be another good one?" I asked my-tree-self.

But no, again I was saddened to see that this orchard was not to be one of my favorites. It was very different from Rich Orchard, which had grown so close to my tree heart. In fact, these trees were very different from all the others.

What do I call these walking trees? They had this strange custom of shaping stone into the likenesses of famous walking trees of the past. They called these trees, "Holywood". There were large stones shaped like the Holywood known for its hard work and others shaped like the one known for its love for our Maker, among many others. There were so many Holywood stones everywhere! So, yes, I call this forest Stone Orchard.

Some trees here had some very good ways. They trusted in our Maker, loved Him, worked very hard for Him by serving others, and, fortunately, they would not give up following Him.

And I heard that they were doing even more now than before! They were so helpful to others, showing real love. Some even patched up my torn bark. You see, some Stone-trees were loving, caring walking trees.

So why isn't this orchard one of my favorites? Stone Orchard lets a fake seer named Jezeltree teach her evil there! Oh, why do they let her teach such darkness among them, letting her pull our Maker's trees away from His light?

Do you remember the last forest we passed through, Castle Orchard? Well, Jezeltree is actively teaching her Stone-tree students to do the evil that Castle-trees had learned themselves from some ancient teachings. She teaches them to bump into others, breaking tree hearts to pieces, and, yes, to offer up sacrifices to Serpothel! How evil Jezeltree is! Why does Stone Orchard let Jezeltree teach her darkness there?!

Of course, Jezeltree's evil students look much like the castle-trees of darkness. They have that gray trunk and red crown of evil. And, yes, they hop about like green hoppers.

But what a terrible surprise! Jezeltree's top students of darkness don't only hop. They also fly! I saw them! Those that learned the deep secrets of darkness fly about as if they are crown-flyers, but they are trees!

Or are they trees? I always had such a fright when these strange, evil trees swooshed by. My bark would go all bumpy, and my crown would stick straight out all around! Fortunately, during the daytime, they usually hid, quietly flying about in the darkness of the forest. And so I could usually avoid them. I wanted nothing to do with those wicked trees of darkness!

Now Stone Orchard also has some real seers, who are true to our Maker. And they have often told Jezeltree and her evil students to stop their evil ways! They tell them that our Maker will bring great suffering upon them all if they do not change, finally striking her evil students with death!

These real seers have another message for the others in Stone Orchard, those who do not hold to Jezeltree's teachings and have not learned the deep secrets of darkness. The seers tell the faithful trees to hold on to what they have until our Maker arrives, to do what pleases our Maker up to the end.

Again, I was very thankful when my roots turned me about one day to take me out of that forest. As was my custom, I called out my farewells, but especially to those who truly walked with our Planter. "Farewell, Brother-trees!"

And these faithful ones said in return, "Farewell, Brother! Be faithful to our Maker!"

I walked through the next dark forest, speaking of our Maker's light while trying my best to avoid Jezeltree's gliders of darkness, and I soon found my-tree-self walking into another clearing.

I thought, "Will this be a good orchard?"

There they were! And just like my dream, they had no faces! "Oh, no! What do I do now? What a sad lot! I won't become like them, will I?"

Still, while shaking a bit, I went out to meet them, these faceless trees walking toward me. As it turned out, they were all walking backward! That's why I couldn't see their faces!

I questioned their strange behavior: "Why, oh why, are you walking backward?!"

"Walking backward? Well, yes, we walk backward when we like and also forward when we like. Every-tree does that. Don't you?"

"Oh, no, I always walk forward."

"How strange!" said the strange tree.

What did these forward-backward walking trees look like? Why, they looked much like any other common walking tree, I suppose. But their faces were green not brown! They were covered over with green moss! How could they even see?! I just don't know.

After some talking and watching, I found that they walked backward only when moving toward the light and forward when leaving the light. You see, they disliked light, though all trees need it to be healthy.

I asked them why they hated the life-giving light, and the answer was always the same: "What? That blinding thing? Who doesn't hate it? How could we even see where we're going if we did face the light?!"

I would try to change the subject, like asking how they liked the weather. But again, we'd get back to their hatred of light.

"It's better not to talk with them," I thought.

But that was easier said than done. Eventually, they would ask where I was from, and I would mention that I had just walked out from the dark forest of strange trees.

"You walk and talk with them? And now you think you can join us? We have nothing to do with that kind, and we will have nothing to do with yours!"

Surprisingly, toward the end of my visit at Death Orchard, I learned that this orchard had some outcasts, some who did not fit in. And what a joy to finally meet them! They were nothing like

their dying brothers in this orchard! They were like
Rich-trees, like the healthy trees of both Castle
Orchard and Stone Orchard!

There were few of these healthy Death-trees.
How happy I was to spend time with them!
Unfortunately, I met them toward the end of my
visit there.

They walked forward all the time! And they
had such lively, healthy faces! I told them, "You few
are so happy! I know you are ready for our Maker's
arrival! Yes, He will be so happy to find you at the
end looking so alive! I feel sorry that I must leave
you so soon."

Though I now had reason to stay there, still,
how happy I was when my roots began to turn me
away from that orchard of death! But I could not
leave without trying to talk some tree-sense into
the moldy faces of the dying trees there. Oh, how
their dull faces and dying wood so saddened me!

"Oh, dying trees, wake up! Yes, you walk
daily, but you walk backward half the day! Why do
you avoid the life-giving light? You are even hiding
behind each other from its warmth! Oh, dying

trees, your faces are a dull green! Turn around and
face the warmth of our Maker's light! Oh, Death
Orchard, wake up from your deathly sleep!"

"Death Orchard?! Ha! We are Life Orchard!
Every forest knows we are very much alive! Ask any
tree! They envy us for our bright, lively look! And
you think you can teach us?! If you would only
listen to us, then you could truly live! But if not,
then return to your strange trees!"

But I just had to say one thing more: "Oh,
Death-trees! Stone Orchard seers say our Maker is
coming one day! And we must please Him to the
end! Oh, Death Orchard, I fear for you! You're not
ready for Him! Wake up and turn your-tree-selves
around toward His life-giving light, before it's too
late! But you few who live for our Maker, keep what
you have! He knows you!"

The dying ones all just turned to go their
way, on their backward way, their moldy, green
faces falling downward. And so ended my
miserable stay with Death Orchard. I was so glad it
was ending! "Farewell, dying trees! Turn to our
Maker's light and live! Oh, farewell, my few living

brothers! Our Maker watches over you!" Now away my roots took me.

But those few living trees called out behind me, "Farewell, our brother! Live for our Maker!"

After a walk and conversation through another dark forest, I found my-tree-self entering the next orchard of walking trees. Can you imagine my joy when I discovered another wonderful orchard, especially after Death Orchard? I really couldn't say what fault this orchard had. I saw none at the time.

These trees walk in the love of the Maker. They patch up torn bark and hurt branches for each other. But they are also quick to patch up the hurts of any strange trees! How wonderful!

Can you guess who they are? They are Love Orchard! And I learn what I can from them. "I love my life here," I often thought. "How I would love to stay here!"

Love Orchard faithfully serves our Maker. I saw Rich-trees walking the strange forests, speaking of our Maker's life-giving light. And I see that here. It seems that nothing can stop these

Love-trees from entering any forest to share the love of our Maker. And many trees of those forests listen with great interest. The light of the Maker is spreading far and wide from this orchard. They even bring His light into a neighboring enemy walking tree forest.

Some-tree might ask, "The neighboring trees are walking trees. How can they belong to an enemy forest and not belong to our Maker's orchard?" Let me explain. Though they are walking trees who speak of the Maker, their tree hearts do not belong to Him. Though they call themselves Maker's Orchard, Love-trees see right through them.

Love Orchard calls this neighboring forest Serp Forest. You see, Serp-trees give their love and service to Serpothel! Yes, they claim to be an orchard of our Maker, knowing what words to speak, but they walk the path of Serpothel not the one of our Maker.

A tree might ask, "How do you know? If they say they are and speak like they are, why then would you say they aren't?" Oh, the troubles, the pain, brought into Love Orchard! Serp Forest sends out such evil trees! And these Serp-trees trouble Love-trees so! Why? Because they faithfully follow our Maker! But, thank our Maker, Love-trees, weak as they are, remain faithful to the Maker, not turning from their love for Him.

Now there are also seers here in Love Orchard. Whereas the Rich-tree seers spoke of trouble in the near future, these seers speak of a great rescue from future troubles! The seers assure us that though we walk in troubles now, we will surely escape the future great trouble coming upon all forests! This is a promise the Maker has made, because we trust Him through our present troubles.

I wondered if this orchard may be my home. Still, I knew the time would come for me to move along. Some of my sapling dreams hadn't yet sprouted.

Even so, I asked from my tree-heart, "Oh, Planter, may this be my home?" However, as expected, my roots soon began to tug at me, pulling me forward again.

"Trees of brotherly love! Please the Planter! Farewell!"

"Farewell, Brother-tree! Return one day!"

And off I went to where my roots would take me, thinking that wherever, who-trees-ever, was before me, it was probably going to be a disappointment, after living among the trees of Love Orchard.

After some conversations while walking through another dark forest of strange trees, I came to another clearing. Nothing could have prepared me for this! These walking trees could hardly walk! They just shuffled round in hopeless circles. Oh, how sad they looked!

They looked much worse off than the dying moss-faced trees! At least Death Orchard could still walk about. These trees must have been like others at one time when they could still freely walk. But now they were covered from crown to ground with earth-crawler like vines. Held in place by those vines, they could only slowly circle around the one way and then circle back the other. They looked so miserable! I wondered, "What happened to these walking trees?! Is there any hope for them?!"

They also had no fruit, unless you count the poisonous red berries of those strangling gray vines. How do I know they were poisonous? I saw a little crown-flyer take a little bite of a red berry. It then chirped, "RRROOOLLLFFF!" as it spit up berry bits, leaving them behind.

I wondered if these were even trees anymore. They didn't look like any I knew of. I even expected to see huge, ugly moths suddenly break free from their cocoons! Oh, how I wished they would escape! How miserable they were!

Did they know their misery? I will tell you of one conversation.

"Why are you like this? What happened?"

"What do you mean, Friend?"

"You're all covered with these strange gray vines."

"What vines?"

"You know, the vines that are strangling you, holding you down. And you're so weak that you can't even produce fruit."

"What do you mean, Friend? There's nothing like a vine on me. But you... you do look a bit strange. Weak? Ha! Never felt better! No fruit? Ha, ha! What are you talking about? Open your eyes! I'm rich with berries! You know, Friend, you must be friendlier than this, if you want to make any friends here."

I know I should have kept quiet and just gone on my way, but I couldn't.

"I can barely see you through these vines! And the fruit's not yours! It's the poison of these vines!"

"Look around. We're the happiest, richest, most fruitful trees of any orchard! We're in need of nothing! Nothing! If you stay, you too will live your best possible tree life!"

It angered me that they wouldn't listen to a word I said! How could they not see how blind they were! If only they would listen to me! So then I decided to speak one more time, but to the whole orchard, about the things I saw.

"Poor, miserable trees! I see you talking to our Maker! But do you know Him as your Maker, the maker of all things? How can a tree tell the Planter anything? Don't tell Him what you want or what is yours! Ask Him! He's the maker of the skies and the earth!

And tell me this! When do you serve Him? I see you busily circling to the left and then to the right and then back all over again! You seem to be so busy looking at whatever it is you're looking at! And you have no fruit, none, nothing to offer Him!

Poor Orchard! I've seen a lot of sick orchards, but yours is the sickest! You are such bad trees! And do you know this? Our Maker is coming soon! What will He do when He finds you walking in circles of poison?! I'm sure He will shout, 'RRROOOLLLFFF,' spit you out, and leave you behind!"

But they all just smiled, and one said, "Poor Orchard? Really? Ha, ha! How funny! We trees are Rich Orchard! You know, Friend, you should be friendlier if you want to stay here with us. And we know you want to stay here. What tree wouldn't? In fact, every tree that plans to just pass through Rich

Orchard finally chooses to stay and make this their home. So be friendly and stay. Become one of us."

"I will never become one of you! But... every tree stays? Really? But why? And why... why would I ever want to become one of you?"

"Well, for one thing, it's clear to all of us that you speak the precious words of our precious Maker. You are such... such a precious teacher! So if you stayed, I'm sure you would become our favorite! What tree is like you, walking that good path, letting nothing turn you from it? Yes, we need a teacher just like you!

Also, here we have all the riches you could ever dream of! We lack nothing here! Nothing! You want lots of precious fruit? We're covered with it! Good health? No orchard is healthier! The best students? They're here, ready to learn from the best! Gold? It's everywhere like the dirt we walk on! A life beyond your wildest tree dreams? It blooms here each day! Friend, don't be the first loser to just pass by all these riches! Tell me! How can you pass up the chance of a lifetime?!"

"Hmmm... Chance of a lifetime? It is sounding pretty good here, now that you've explained it some. I'd be your favorite teacher? Do you really think so? Gold? I don't know what I'd do with it, but it is pretty, and you sure have a lot of it! And I guess it wouldn't hurt to stay for my health. Health is important, after all. And you do look happy here. Hmmm... Let me think...

Covered with fruit? Oh, I was going to say something about that, but I can't remember what it was. My crown just suddenly grew cloudy. What was it?"

"Precious teacher, yes, stay here and be covered in fruit! Become one of us!"

All the trees now joined in with a cheer, "Become one of us! Become one of us! Become one of us!"

My bark was now getting happy bumps all over! It's so nice to feel needed! Also, how wonderful it is to have so many tree wishes answered, and all in the same place! Of course, I pinched my-tree-self to see if I was dreaming. I wondered, "Could this really be home? Everything is right here!" I couldn't believe my knots! "What luck!" I thought.

I looked about at all the cheering trees before me and said, "Well... I'm so surprised! It is so hard to say 'no' to so much! It really is... You offer me so very much here!"

Now I still had something on my branches, and though all knots were on me, I stopped a moment to try to remember what it was, "What was it? Covered with fruit... Covered with fruit... Now, what was I thinking? What was it? Oh, yeah! Now I remember! It was... It was about poison, wasn't it?"

Now with my branches clearing some, coming out from the clouds, I turned to this welcoming and cheering orchard and said, "I'm sorry. I think I shouldn't. I don't think I should stay."

There then sprouted a great rumbling of mumblings.

But I continued, "You see, I visited other orchards before yours, like Rich and Love. I was having a hard time remembering just now, but I think they were pretty good too. You know, they have a lot of fruit too.

So I think I really must be going now. I think I've stayed here long enough. But thank you every-tree for the kind offers. We'll see... Maybe later... So I'll see you..."

I very slowly turned to leave but finally found I couldn't! I couldn't take even one step! And I couldn't see a thing! I was blind! Oh, the shock! I felt the vines twisting round and round my trunk, tighter and tighter, crawling up toward my crown! They were strangling me! I was now tightly bound to the golden ground of Poor Orchard! I couldn't move but in a poor circle!

Forests of questions raced through my crown: "Are these zomtrees? I thought they were... Am I a zomtree? How could this happen to me? Oh, why, oh, why did I stay so long?"

Now the rumbling of mumblings was fading away as I entered a quiet dream world. I turned and saw my future self! He was standing on the poisoned path before me, bound by evil gray vines! Those vines were holding him prisoner to his gold!

My future self was an old, ugly gray tree, covered with poison berries! I watched him as he circled around the one way and then the other.

Sadly, he could not see how miserable he was. He tried to smile while looking at all the shiny gold scattered about him. There was so little dirt for him to stand on! Trees, you know, need dirt to survive!

But then my future self thought, "I'm healthy and rich! I have it all! So why do I have an empty heart? Why must I pretend this happiness? Why?! There is no reason! I have need of nothing! Nothing! I have all I want! So why am I just a hollow tree? What am I missing? Who am I missing?"

I saw a Love-tree walking by my future self. He was calling out, "Poor trees, your Maker loves you! You say you have all you need, all you want! But you don't know that you are nothing without Him! Nothing!

Even now, your Maker is nearby, calling you! Can't you hear His voice? Turn to Him, and

He will walk with you and you with Him! Listen now! He's calling your name!"

My poor, future self turned toward me, yet was unable to see. You see, he was blind! He tried stepping out in my direction, but those vines held him tight! He began to cry in misery, "My Maker is calling my name? What is my name? I have no name!"

The Planter was standing nearby. He quietly called out, "Homer."

That old tree was shaken. He answered, "I hear Your voice!"

My future self on that poisoned path was now fading fast, and then was gone! My present, miserable self was now left standing alone.

Again, the Planter, standing nearby, said, "Homer."

I answered, "My Planter, I turn to You." As I pointed blind knots up toward above the sky, I moaned, "Oh, my Maker, forgive me. Forgive my wandering heart.

But now I remember! Yes, I remember! I judged these poor trees! I called them bad! But who knows the heart but You? You alone are Judge! I was wrong! Oh, my Maker, I turn to You! May I walk together with You again..."

Suddenly, they came! I smelled a forest of hungry-runners! And I could smell the dust flying about! And I thought, "Oh no! What is this?! What is happening now?!"

But I now saw the dust flying, the dust of a hundred hungry-runners! I could see again! I was no longer blind! But I wondered, "Why are they here? Why now?" You see, though now I could see, I knew I was still in very big trouble! These hungry-runners were very hungry!

Poor Orchard was crying out in misery upon misery! But not once did I hear them ask our Maker for help. They were telling Him this or claiming that of Him but not ever asking! Oh, what miserable trees they were!

But now I had hope! With the help of several hungry-runners, I was pulling myself free from those clinging vines! But, of course, I wondered, "How will I escape the disappearing branches of a hundred hungry-runners?!"

I thank our Planter who watches over all, even over a foolish tree like me! There was King-runner! He was there! "Did he follow me here? But how can he disappear a hundred of these?!" I questioned.

Now, a forest of king-runners was arriving! They were more than the number of my branches, even more than my leaves! And they were running about everywhere, quickly disappearing hungry-runners! And so along with the miserable cries of wretched Poor-trees, there were now the squeals, the shrieks, and the gurglings of hungry-runners, as they disappeared either into hungry king-runners or into dark forests!

This was my chance to escape! I carefully walked through the flowing sap of trees and runners, clear sap mixing with red, as I walked straight for that light ahead.

I thought, "Thank Planter! That nightmare is over! I'm walking home again!" Then turning, looking up past the sky, I said, "Thank You, my Planter, for forgiving me, this foolish tree! You freed me from a useless, circling life of a zomtree!

But oh... our Maker, free Poor Orchard, please!"

3

LIVING DREAM HILL

With no chance of saying farewell, I was thankfully on my way home through another dark forest of strange trees. I spoke again of the light of our Planter and of being thankful to Him. Many listened. Soon I was exiting this dark forest. And I could see the light before me.

And there it was! The hill of my dreams, right there before me! My roots quickly took me up to the top of that hill and then set me down near the center, with me waiting. But waiting for what? What was it that my sapling dreams showed me of this hill? Could I remember? I tried, but the memory walked away, keeping its distance. Still, I knew this: "I can rest here from my travels."

Some seasons of sunshine and rain passed by there on dream hill. But one day, there before me up in the sky were these great clouds of flying flowers. And I thought, "How wonderful! But what season of new beginnings could this be? Am I finally walking home?" Well, I soon learned the answer.

I suddenly knew that some-tree was climbing my hill. Who could it be? What? It was me? No, it couldn't be! I was right here, wasn't I?

But, you see, she looked so much like me. She was a walking tree! Then I knew. It was her, my would-be, soon-to-be wife! She climbed to the top of Dream Hill and stood near me! Then she told me her name, "Hello. My name is Evening."

"Hello. Some call me 'Me-tree', but I think that's not a real name."

She laughed, "You don't have a name?"

"Well, not yet, I guess. The strange trees I grew up with called me 'Grandson'. Do you have any ideas for my name? There must be a better one than 'Me-tree' or 'Grandson'."

"Well, let's see... Me-tree, what's your dream?"

"Let's see... Home! Ever since I was a little sapling, my dream has been to finally walk home."

"So your dream has been home... walking home? You've been a home-walker all these seasons? Home-walker... Hmmm... Oh! How about Homer?! That's short for Home-walker!"

"Wow! I didn't know that was really my name! That's what our Maker called me in Poor Orchard!"

"Our Maker called you Homer?"

"Yes, first in a zomtree dream and then in a real circle of poison."

"Zomtree dream? Circle of poison?"

"Oh, that's all behind me now. Thank our Maker! Evening, I'll tell you about that soon. But

Homer? That's really my name? I guess it is! Wow!
I'm Homer! Evening, thank you!"

"Oh, don't thank me! Thank our Maker! Say,
glad to meet you, Homer!"

"Glad to meet you, Evening!"

"Oh, Homer, just call me 'Eve'. That's short
for 'Evening'."

"Okay, Eve."

And so to make a short story even shorter,
after the usual time of engagement and the
traditional walking-tree wedding ceremony,
witnessed by at least two crown-flyers, we became
husband and wife. We two were very happy on
Dream Hill. But what could possibly happen next?
As you know, a tree's life is always changing. And
my tree life isn't any different.

Well, several seasons later, he appeared. He
grew right up out of the earth between us. He was
our son! He was such a tiny walking seedling! And
we were about to name him when, suddenly, the
rays of the sun shined brightly upon our little
seedling-son.

"Look!" Eve said. "We've got a name for him!"

"Sunray?" I asked.

Eve liked it, but she thought it was a bit long. So she said, "How about shortening his name to 'Ray'?"

"Yes," I said. "That's his name then, 'Ray'."

Well, it wasn't long that Ray's height caught up with his mother's and mine, and he even came to pass us up some time later. How proud we were. Our son Ray stood quite tall there between us.

The three of us were quite happy on Dream Hill, which was good, because none of us at the time could walk away from Dream Hill, even if we had wanted to. It seemed that the good Planter had planted us here to stay.

Ray, several times, even reminded us, his parents, "Home's the place you'd never leave, even if you ever could!" Of course, His mother and I agreed. We were so proud of him. Ray had learned well.

But still... there were my dreams. And dreams, somehow or other, you know, have a way of just suddenly and surely breaking into the day-to-day life of a happy tree. And so many seasons later, it happened.

"Look! What are these?! Are they the walking grass seeds of your dreams, Father?!"

"I think they are, Son. Look at them spin about and walk! Look! Now, they're planting themselves!"

And they grew right there, there on our Dream Hill. And I quietly thought to my-tree-self, "We'll be walking home soon."

But no-tree, no matter how much sap flows through its trunk, could ever foresee what would happen next... No, no-tree.

"Father, Mother, what are those? They're coming our way!"

I said, "Son, I've seen them before. Let's hope they pass by. Family, let's ask Planter for help, 'Our Planter, please protect us.'"

"Father, are they very bad?"

"Yes, Son, they are. Be quiet now. Family, let's ignore them."

But those three tree-climbers still climbed our Dream Hill anyway. And they went straight to work, climbing each of us, disappearing leaves, branches, turning our Dream Hill into a Nightmare Hill, our three crowns falling apart, falling into pieces, crowns disappearing into hungry tree-climbers.

"Oh, Planter, when will they stop? We are so small!" I cried.

But they kept tearing off leaves, branches, disappearing all.

"Oh, why is this happening to my family? Why now? Help…" I whispered while looking up past the empty sky. And then just as quickly as those tree-climbers had arrived, they left. But now, we had very little of our-tree-selves left.

"Father, Mother, both of you have only a few branches left, only on the top."

"Yes, Son," I said. "You also."

"Will we live, Father?"

"I think we will," I said.

"We will," said Mother. "We still have our roots."

I said, "And we still have our top branches. Thank Planter for that."

"But I feel so plain now, so empty. We are all so... so poor." Ray began to sob. And trees rarely cry.

"Don't worry. It will all grow back, Ray," said his mother.

I said, "Family, we must trust our Planter. He has His plans, which we cannot understand. Trust Him. We can trust Him."

I looked Ray's way: "Ray, how many times was I nearly disappeared by hungry-runners?"

"Was it three times?" asked Ray.

"I think it was three times... And, Ray, how many times did our Maker rescue me?"

"Every time, Dad."

"Yes, Ray. Every time. Ray, we can trust our Maker with this time, too."

"Yes, Dad. That's right. We can trust our Maker."

Eve said, "Yes, we can."

And I said, "Yes, Family, we can, and we will."

Now the next morning, three very strange visitors came to Dream Hill. They were the two-rooted kind. But I didn't think they were the woodsmen I had heard about. They weren't carrying anything that I thought might be an axe, nothing that looked dangerous. Besides, what harm could any woodsmen do us now? Things could never get worse than this. This I knew. Call it "tree-sense" if you like. And, of course, every tree has it. In other words, I wasn't too, too worried about these visitors.

I couldn't even begin to explain what happened or what was said. But since then, I have become friends with a two-rooter, and he was kind enough to find that strange family of three and ask them about their visit to Dream Hill.

Though the following short story doesn't make a bit of tree-sense, my hope is that non-trees, at least, might get something from it. What follows are the very words of those three strange visitors, as reported by my two-rooter friend. Please read with a tree's patience:

"The family of three looked up and saw Dream Hill.

"Look! What are those?" said the little girl.

"Three crosses? Hmmm... I have a book of three crosses at home. Oh, I remember. I used to read that book under my blanket at night, using just a flashlight. Ha!"

"But why were you hiding under your blanket, Daddy?"

"Maybe we'll talk about that later, Little One."

"Hmmm... I don't think they're crosses," said Mother.

"What's a cross?" asked Jill.

"Oh, your father can tell you later," said Mother.

"Well, Dorothy, how about we three look at that book of three crosses together?"

"Yes, can we, Daddy? Mommy, can we?"

"Well, I don't know. Maybe if I'm home. We'll see..."

"Oh, Mommy, you're never home!"

Father said, "Well, let's go look at that hill. What could those cross-looking things be?"

"Oh, I don't think I will. You two run along without me. Tell me if they're crosses, but I doubt it. I haven't seen a cross for years."

"Oh, Mommy, please climb the hill with us. Please..."

"Oh, okay. But let's make it quick. I have an important appointment."

"You do?" asked Father.

"Yes, I do."

"Hmmm..."

"Mommy! Daddy! Let's climb the hill of three... of three crosses! Let's go!"

The family of three climbed Dream Hill.

"Mommy! Look! Are those crosses?!"

"No, they aren't, Sweetie. They're palm trees. A palm tree from the side looks a lot like a cross when it just has few branches. They must have been hit by a storm."

"Hmmm... I haven't heard of any big storms out here for a while," said Father.

Mother continued, "Of course, there aren't any crosses around here anymore."

"Why, Mommy? What happened to them?"

"Ask your father, Sweetie."

"We'll tell you when we get home, Kido," said Father.

Father continued, "You know, Family, I think these are the walking palm trees I've heard about. Look at all their roots. Most of their roots are above ground. Look! Their trunks don't even touch the ground! That's how they can walk!"

"You mean they walked up this hill?" asked Jill.

"Looks like they did, Kido. I don't see any others around here."

"They walked up here for us! I know they did! It was just for our family!"

"Ha, ha! Well, okay, Sweetie, if you want to think so," said Mother. "But scientists say the walking palm tree is a fairy tale, you know, like Cinderella."

"Well, it could be true," said Father. "Many witnesses have seen them walking, and there are some videos…"

"See, Mommy! They walked up this hill just for our family! And they look like crosses! Oh, Daddy! Tell me about crosses!"

"Okay… but let's head home. We'll look at that book of three crosses, and then you'll know all about them."

"Okay! Bye, bye, my three friends, my tree friends! I love you!"

"Ha, ha!" laughed Mother.

"Ha, ha, that's cute, Kido," said Father.

The family of three made their way back down Dream Hill. They had an important appointment with the book of three crosses, a once-in-a-lifetime appointment."

Thank you for your patience, my tree readers. I know my two-rooter friend did his best to tell this story. Please understand that it was not meant to make much sense to a tree. Later, I will work on a better translation. And so our tree's tale continues…

"Father, what were those... those strange creatures walking on two roots?"

"Well, they do look very similar to the woodsmen I've heard about, but I don't know much about them. Our Planter has made some pretty wonderful creatures, hasn't He? Ask your mother."

"Mother, do you know about these things on two roots?"

"Like your father, I've heard something about them, but not much. Maybe we can ask others more about them when we get home. I'm sure we'll learn more about these wonderful creatures there."

"Home? We're not home?"

"No, Son. Don't you remember I told you of my dreams from when I was just a sapling? Remember the dream of me-we-three? You, your mom, and I walk down from Dream Hill, walking home. Eve, you remember, don't you?"

"Yes, of course. We three will soon be going down this hill, walking home."

The walking-seed grasses were by now quite tall and green, and they were waving in the cool breeze.

I said, "Look! The walking grasses are waving 'Good-bye'. It must be time to walk home!"

"Oh... but Father... where is home? You told us of five sick orchards and two healthy ones, Rich and Love. Oh, may we live in a healthy orchard?"

"Well..."

"You said Love Orchard isn't that far from here. Can't that be home?"

"In fact, Son, our Planter... Mother?"

Eve continued, "Our Planter told us, Ray, where home is. And yes, it's Love Orchard! Homer, we're walking home!"

"Yes!" said Ray. "Love Orchard's home!"

Now a little crown-flyer appeared, seemingly from nowhere.

"Oh, Family! This is Sky-ranger!"

"Chirp! Greetings Earth-watcher and family!"

The family greeted Sky-ranger, "Greetings!"

"Chirp! A message from our Maker! 'You three will walk to your home away from home, but there will be some delay. Do not fear. I am with you, says your Maker.' Farewell, Earth-watchers! Walk well! Chirp!"

The family called out to Sky-ranger as she flitted away.

"Farewell, little crown-flyer!"

"Farewell, Friend!"

"Farewell, Sky-ranger!"

"What does 'home away from home' mean?" I thought out loud.

"Our true home must be up there beyond the sky with our Planter," answered Eve.

"Yes!" said Ray. "But how will we walk there?"

Every-tree had a short laugh, "Ha, ha, ha!"

I said, "Our Maker knows what He's doing."

It was then that our roots began growing downward, even now taking we three down Dream Hill, pulling us back along the path which I had walked many seasons before. I and my family were now walking home, or so I thought.

"Which way, Homer?"

"Follow the light, Family."

"Father! Look! Up in the sky! What's that?!
Is it a crown-flyer?!"

"I don't know, Son. I've never seen one! Eve,
do you know?"

"Never seen anything like it. But it... it looks
like a flying tree!"

"Mother, Father, look! There's a two-rooter
sitting on it! And it's waving a branch at us!"

"Just ignore it, Son. Maybe it'll go away. No-
tree look."

The flying tree and its rider were soon
buzzing away along the path.

Ray said, "He's flying away!"

"Good!" I said. "We just had to ignore him.
See?"

But before a tree could say, "The rain falls
upon every-tree," there was that buzzing again.

"Look! Tree-flyer's back! I knew it!" shouted
Ray. "Oh! Now, the two-rooter is waving both
branches at us! Look, Father, Mother!"

"Just ignore them," I whispered. "Don't look."

"But I think they're friendly," suggested Eve.

"I think so too. I'll wave back! Hey!!! Hey!!!" hollered Ray while waving his branches.

The flying tree now began to quickly tilt its wood-self side to side, first to the left and then to the right, and back again.

I wondered, "What's it doing? Is it friendly? Maybe not."

I shouted, "Ray! Don't do that! Don't wave at them!"

"Oh! They're coming this way! And fast! Father, should we ignore them?!"

The flying tree and its rider were now diving straight for us!

I quickly whispered, looking up beyond the sky, "Please, help us." And then turning to Ray, I shouted, "No! Don't ignore them! Family, jump! NOW!!!"

We quickly jumped toward the nearby cliff, the flying tree barely missing us! And so we three rolled over that cliff, and now we were falling! Just as we reached the roots of that cliff, dust began flying everywhere!

"Reeeiii! Reeeiiireeeiiireeeiii!!! Reeeiii!"

I guessed that many hungry-runners were racing along the path right past us! There must have been hundreds of them! For a long time, they just kept running past us on the path. Thank our Maker! They didn't see us!

"Father, what's that terrible smell?"

"Hungry-runners, Son. Hundreds of them. Quiet now."

It seemed like it took the time it takes for a seedling to break out from its seed, an eternity. These hungry runners ran past us forever. But finally, the runners were gone, taking their dust with them.

"Okay, Family, I think we're safe now."

"Homer, that flying tree saved our lives."

"Yes, I know."

"Tree-flyer saved us! Yeah!!!" shouted Ray.

I looked upward and said, "We thank you, our Planter!"

And Eve said, "Yes, we thank you, Planter!" Turning to me, she said, "Homer, let's thank Tree-flyer too, when we can."

"Yes," I said. "We should thank the flying tree trunk, too."

"Father, Mother, I don't see Tree-flyer! He's gone! Will he return?"

"Maybe, Son. Let's listen for its buzzing sound."

Ray cheered, "Tree-flyer saved our family! He's my hero!"

"Tree-flyer?" I asked. "I thought we might call him 'Swoopertrunk'."

"Why, Honey?" asked Eve.

"Well, that flying tree trunk swooped down and made us jump off that cliff, and it..."

Eve interrupted, "...swooped down to rescue us."

"I don't know, Dad. 'Swoopertrunk' sounds kind of corny to me."

"Okay, okay, Tree-flyer it is..."

"Yes! Tree-flyer!!!"

"...for now."

"Homer…"

"Well, I'd like to meet the flying trunk and get to know him some before we call him our hero. He couldn't be on the side of the hungry-runners, could he?"

"Father, really?"

"Just saying… What decent tree goes flying around the sky without its crown while carrying a waving two-rooter?"

Eve said, "Well, what decent tree goes walking around the forests without a name while talking with strange trees?"

"You got my branches there, Darling. Still, I'd like to meet the flying trunk."

"Tree-flyer!" exclaimed Ray.

"Oh, there was something on my branches," I said. "Family, what were we doing before we met Tree-flyer and all those smelly hungry-runners?"

"We were walking home!"

Mother said, "That's right, Ray, we were. Homer, we're walking home!"

"Home! Yeah! What?! What's that buzzing sound?!"

"Ha! Bees, Father! Ha, ha, ha! Bees!"

"Ha, ha, ha!"

"He, he, he!"

But still, there was that faint, distant buzzing sound. Of course, I had every-tree ignore it, and we again walked on our way home.

"We're going home!" exclaimed Ray.

4

A GRAY WORM'S CASTLE

I had walked seven orchards and lived Dream Hill,
finding Eve and Ray. And then together as a family
we faced the dangers of tree climbers, the visit of
three two-rooters, and the frights of a flying tree
trunk and its smelly mob of hungry-runners. But
now my family was finally in a place of peace.

As the reader must have guessed, I and my
tree family were welcomed into Love Orchard. We
finally arrived here after some careful walking
through Poor Orchard. Oh, how my family loves it

here! When we first got here, Ray was learning the ways of Love Orchard, Eve was making many close friends, and Love Orchard recognized me, Homer, as a teacher of our Maker's words.

We three were very happy and at peace here at our home away from home, and I really did think my tree's tale would end about here with those happy tree words, *happily ever after*. In fact, we and our friends were sure of it, and so we happily celebrated those happy tale-end words, and were still celebrating for some time. But...

...you must have noticed that if a tree is, unfortunately, cut across from one side to the other, its trunk is made up of circles within circles. And so it seems to be that a common tree's life is also made up of these circles within circles. That, in a nutshell, is the story of my common walking tree life.

You see, my life circled back around to even more tree dreams. Earlier, I had three sapling dreams, but now as a tree, I had three more. Of course, I told my dreams to those around me, both family and friends, but no-tree understood what they meant.

Actually, every-tree felt that my tree dreams sounded a lot like treeberish. I cannot fault them for this. Indeed, that is what they seemed. But, still, I will let the reader read my dreams to consider what they mean, before continuing with my common walking tree's tale.

My first dream: I was rolling round and round, going everywhere yet nowhere. The rolling made me feel sick. I wondered, "How can I roll around like a piece of fruit? I'm a tree not fruit." And then a thought: "What?! I'm not a tree?!" Next, I was flying through sky and deep waters until I hit earth. I looked around. There! A pile of dead trees! I asked my-tree-self, "But what can I do?"

My second dream: An ugly gray worm was laughing at me. But some two-rooters with beast heads were pulling me toward purple water. Suddenly, three of the two-rooters became fiery yellow wood! I was falling now past purple flames, the yellow burning wood leading the way! But now,

I was flying through white clouds! I thought, "I'm safe now! But who's carrying me?"

My third dream: I was standing around with many walking trees. We were listening to an old tree talk and talk. As it talked, the old tree's crown dropped off and burst into flames! And there it was! An earth-crawler's head was sticking out from the tree's trunk! Then that ugly crawler burst into flames! It was dead, and I was happy! But I wondered, "Will they kill me now?"

Like I said, I told my three dreams to those around me, but no-tree could tell me what they meant. So, of course, I thought I would just ignore the dreams. But I just couldn't get them out of my crown, though I tried.

You see, they were making me think only of them. I couldn't even think about what I was teaching. One day, I planned to teach something about the meaning of tree life, but I began by saying, "Don't listen to an earth-crawly in a tree!"

All but my best students nodded in agreement. But I then stopped my-tree-self and added, "Trees, today we'll discuss the meaning of tree life." And then all but my best students sat there with looks of complete understanding.

I did get through the lesson okay that day. But afterward I found my wife and said, "Eve, I can't get those dreams out of my crown! I shouted something about an earth-crawler in a tree today in class! What am I doing?! Eve, I've got to do better than this! But what can I do?!"

"Maybe you need to learn the meaning of those dreams. Take a little vacation?"

"Maybe you're right. Let's think about that."

We talked about it more and decided that I would search out the meaning of my dreams. I had to get them behind me. I had to move on with my tree life.

The next morning, I said my farewells: "I'll be back in a couple moons. See you soon, Eve, Ray. I love you two!"

"Yes, Honey. Stay safe. Go where you must to put your dreams to rest. And come home soon! Love you!"

"See you soon! Love you, Dad!"

"Bye for now! Love Orchard, see you!"

Every-tree called out a farewell, and I walked along on my way, sap somehow clouding my seeing knots.

I decided to walk to my first home. I thought, "I've got to ask Grandad. I hope he doesn't mind."

After a long walk past many forests and orchards, I arrived at home #1. When Grandad saw me coming, he rumbled with joy, "Surprise, Grandson!!! Welcome home! Welcome to your first home!"

And all the trees of the forest cheered and shouted out to me, "Surprise!!! Welcome home, Grandson!!!"

"Oh, thanks, Grandad! Thank you, every-tree! It's good to be back! But it's only for a visit!"

"Yes, of course," said Grandad. "We understand, Grandson. Well, we don't really understand, but we try to understand, so we must be understanding. Trees don't walk away from home, you know. But welcome home, Grandson!"

"Yes, I understand," I said.

You see, we trees have a very hard time hiding our feelings and thoughts from other trees. Of course, we are quite shy with non-trees and don't think or say a thing around them, usually, that is.

"Grandad, I have something to ask you."

"Yes, Grandson. What is it?"

"Grandad, you didn't want to hear any more of my dreams, but it's been so long since I left home, and you are my Grandad. So do you think I can tell you another dream and ask you what it might mean?"

"Another dream, Grandson?"

"Well... three dreams."

"Three? Well... Maybe. But tell me, Grandson. What became of your first three dreams? Did any of them happen?"

"Yes, Grandad."

"All three?"

"Yes, Grandad. All three."

"I see. Well, that does make a difference then. Yes, Grandson. Tell me your dreams. I will try to help."

I told Grandad all three dreams. And he listened carefully to each one. I hoped he would. And then I said, "Grandad, what do you think?"

"Think?! What do I think?! How can I think like this?! Your dreams are not common tree dreams! But, Grandson, I can say something."

"Yes, Grandad?"

"Even if your grandad doesn't know what your dreams mean, he can tell you, Grandson, that you will live through things that your Grandad and all these trees here never did and never will. Your tree life never even passed through our crowns, Grandson.

You're rolling and flying? A little gray worm is laughing at you? An earth-crawler is faking it's a tree? No, Grandson. The meaning of your dreams is not for me to tell you. Grandson, you are a young walking tree, and I'm just an old standing tree."

"But Grandad! You did! You told me! A crawler is faking it's a tree! Yes, Grandad! I think that's it! Thank you, Grandad!"

"Oh, okay, Grandson. I'm glad I could help some, but that is only one dream. But I can add this."

"Yes, Grandad."

"Grandson, find another tree like yourself, another walking tree. Find an elder walking tree. You must have elders, don't you? Ask your elder the meaning of your dreams, Grandson."

"Yes, Grandad! That's right! I'll look for an elder walking tree!"

"Good, Grandson! Get some help from an elder of your own kind! Now, go on walking! Ha! My grandson is a walking tree! Ha, ha! Go walking now! Ha, ha, ha!!!"

"Yes, Grandad! Thank you! I'll come back for a visit! Farewell!!!"

"Farewell, Grandson! Yes, come visit! And Grandson, be careful!!! Watch out for ugly earth-crawlers hiding in trees!!!"

All the neighbors suddenly gasped, "GAAASSSPPP!!!"

I called out farewells to all the neighbors as I walked along, and they sent their return farewells.

As I left, I could hear the rumblings of their whisperings grow louder and louder.

But then a great thunder burst out above them all: "Return safely, Grandson!!!"

And I shouted back from the top of my branches: "Yeah!!! Grandad!!!"

Then I asked my-tree-self, "Where can I find an elder walking tree? Not at Love Orchard. I can't say "good-bye" again. That was hard enough. And besides, I asked most every tree there already. But where then?"

So I had to stop to do some deep tree thinking. "Which way am I to go?" I thought.

And then I got it! "The first orchard! Loveless Orchard! The first orchard must be the oldest one! It must have an elder tree! It must!"

And so I was off to see an elder, the wisest of the orchards. "But will Loveless Orchard welcome me?" I thought. "And will the elder be willing to talk to me?"

After a good, long walk, I arrived at Loveless Orchard. Of course, they were all walking in their line, with most listening and few talking.

I asked some older trees, "Is a wise elder tree here?"

The tree at the back of the line answered, "All we walking trees came from the land of sunrises. That's what I was told when I was young. You might find your wise elder there."

I said, "Thank you very much, Friend!"

And he said, "I'm just telling the truth. Let's not take it to be more than that!"

"Yes," I said. "Thank you!"

I left before the mumbling in the line got any louder. I was happy. That was what I was looking for, a direction. Now, I had a plan for finding a wise elder, someone to tell me the meaning of my dreams. Though many trees believe life's answers are found in sunsets, I was now planning a walk into the distant sunrise.

Early the next morning, the sun was just peaking over some distant mountains. "This is it," I thought. "Now, I'm off to find a wise elder walking tree. He must be out there. He has to be. After all, all we walking trees came from there."

And so with the sunrise there before me, I started out on my final journey. I was stepping out toward a golden land, a place where I knew my dreams could hide no longer.

I walked through many dark forests of strange trees, listening to their whisperings everywhere I turned, doing my tree best to walk my straight line for where the sun had risen. And as I walked along, I gathered courage from our Maker. I found the courage to continue walking those dark forests. I even found the courage to speak to these strange trees the words of our Maker. I told them to trust in Him, to look up to Him for help.

Now I suddenly noticed that a crowd of crows were perched throughout the branches of this forest. I hadn't seen any till now. They saw that I saw them, and so they began to call out with a deafening sound: "CAW! CAW! CAAAW!!!"

I looked round and saw some four-rooters trying to cover their sound openings as they raced off in every direction. But I did not have such freedom as these. I continued walking on my way in my sunrise direction, as best I could. I was aiming toward where I guessed the sun would rise the next morning.

I saw that many crows were now speeding off to places unknown. I told myself, "No doubt they are flying off to a place no good for me-tree." But what else could I do but to continue on the direction set before me? I walked onward, in search of the meaning of my dreams.

Soon there were two-rooters with beastly heads all about me in that dark forest. I stopped and did not make another move. "Oh, these are the beasts of my second dream!" I told my-tree-self. "So soon? Is my second dream first?!" I put my trust in our Maker.

How strange they were! Some of these beastly two-rooters had thick branches shooting upward from their heads, one bigger branch followed by a smaller one. Some had heads covered with thin roots, their hungry openings filled with great disappearing branches. Others had the heads of crows. And there were still other ugly ones, with their own beastly heads.

I had stopped where I was when I saw them, trying very hard to look like just another tree. They were all running about here and there, looking for something. Yes, I wondered if they were looking for me. How happy I was that my plan to just stop and ignore them was working.

But then all the crows of the trees began pointing their disappearing branches right at me! "Oh, no!" I thought, probably a little too loudly. It was bad enough that I was in a strange dark forest. But now, I was at the center of a dark, cawing crow storm!

I placed one root forward, but then the ugly beasts quickly came up to me and picked me up in their branches. Off we were now, racing out of one dark forest into an even darker one. "Oh, what will become of me? What will become of my dreams?! Oh, Maker! Help!"

Up ahead, I could see a dark castle. I remembered what Sky-ranger, my trusted friend, had told me. I thought, "Could this be the evil castle of Stanamon?! Oh, Maker! Help!"

The ugly beasts quickly carried me into the castle and dropped me on the ground. At first, I couldn't see anything in this dark place. But soon I could see a black and gray thing sitting on a pile of dead trees. "It must be Stanamon sitting on his throne," I thought.

Just like Sky-ranger had said, he was all covered in black, his gray twisted face standing out. I thought, "His seeing knots don't line up quite right. He's so twisted, and... he's an ugly gray. Is this the ugly gray worm of my second dream?"

Stanamon said, "What?"

I remained quiet there before him on the floor, quietly thinking what I should do. I was still trying to look like any other tree.

Stanamon spoke again: "So you are the walking tree that speaks of light! Haaa! Speak of light now! I'm listening! Ha! Ha! Haaa!!!"

I kept quiet, trying to ignore him.

But then he shouted, "Trying to ignore me?! Ignore me now!!!"

He held up a sharp, shiny thing, bringing it down on several of my roots.

I shouted, "Owwweee!!! That hurts!"

"The tree speaks!"

I said, "Owww... Is that why I'm here? Because I speak of our Maker's light? Of course, I'm happy to tell you of his light. You see..."

"Silence, ugly pencil!"

Later, I learned what a pencil is. Stanamon was very ignorant, calling me, a walking tree, a pencil. But how could such evil be anything but ignorant?

Stanamon started shouting all about: "You ugly beasts! Finally, you follow commands?! Go along now to the kitchen for a snack! No, not you, Snabeast! Stay here! Help me with this pile of dead wood!"

"Ssss!"

I thought, "How ignorant he is, calling me dead wood!" But then my tree thoughts continued, "Oh, no! What will become of me? He thinks I'm dead wood?! What now?! Will I see my family again?" I did my best to look up from that dark castle, up past the sky: 'Oh, our Maker! Please may I not end like this! What of my other dreams?!

Shouldn't I walk through them too, even if they are as ugly as this Stanamon?! Oh, Planter, please rescue me!"

"Ugly as who?! Rescue?!" shouted Stanamon. "Haaa! Look around! There's no one here to rescue you, Deadwood!!!"

I shouted, "I'm not dead wood!"

"Wait and see, talking pencil! Let's see how your wood likes fire!"

I shouted back, "Fire?! Trees stomp out fires! We hate fire!"

"Ha, ha, ha!!!"

Stanamon walked over to the pool of water, while Snabeast tightly held on to me. Stanamon called out, "Lord Serpothel! I have some dead wood here for you! And it's ready to meet you! Lord Serpothel?!"

"Silence, Worm!!! Do you think I don't know?!"

Stanamon stepped back from the pool a few steps, and just then purple flames burst upward, hitting the stone castle ceiling.

"Stanamon, you've had your fun with that dead wood of the light! Now, send it down to me! Walking tree, do you like light?! Well, what about bright red fire?! Haaa!!!"

"Haaa! Haaa! Haaa!!!" laughed the two holding on to me.

Stanamon was now trying to pull me toward the pool. Looking to Snabeast, he shouted, "Fool! Don't just stand there! Help me get this to Lord Serpothel!!!"

"Ssss! Yes, King!!!"

I could feel my-tree-self shaking with fear as Snabeast and Stanamon tried dragging me to the flaming pool.

I looked upward again: "Oh, Maker, help!"

"Haaa! Deadwood of the light! You're shaking! Haaa! Your Maker can't help you now! Haaa! How useless is your dead light! Oh, maybe you could have been of some use to the darkness... But too late now, and no great loss!"

Turning toward the kitchen, Stanamon shouted, "Crobeast! Rhibeast! Swibeast! Get over here!!!"

"Reeeiii!"

"Caaaw!"

"Ghiiihhh!"

I was shaking all over with fear, which must have made it difficult for them to hold on to me. But now with the help of three more beasts, Stanamon was dragging me closer to that purple, flaming pool. But still I was grabbing at anything I could get my roots on, anything that could stop me from reaching that pool of fire.

"Oh, my Maker... please help..."

We reached the pool, and Stanamon shouted one last thing, "No help for you! Here! Stomp out this fire!!!"

They then pushed me over into that pool of flames, my roots still reaching out to grab anything they could. So I pulled three of them in with me, but I didn't know which ones. For the three quickly burst into flames, turning into nothing but yellow branches. I think Sky-ranger once called them "skeletons". These three skeletons began sinking in the flaming pool. Then quickly they were racing toward the bottom. And I... I was following close behind them!

"Oh, Maker, help..."

I was quickly trailing behind the three. There they were! They had flames trailing behind them, but I didn't see any flames on me. "Not yet," I thought. "Is someone keeping me safe from the fire?"

We were falling for a while. Everything around us was a deep purple, but sometimes there were bursts of red because of the flames from the skeletons.

"What will become of me-tree? Is this the end?"

Below us, I could see something like an ugly under-earth crawler! It was purple with some red. It had strange roots and branches all over, all in the wrong places. "What an ugly crawler!" I thought. "Is that Serpothel down there? Is he waiting for me-tree?"

He seemed to be laughing while thundering up toward me: "Come here!!! Yes, here!!!"

I was drawing my roots up closer to me, not knowing what else to do. We were falling fast toward the bottom, even now almost there!

But then... Something grabbed me from behind! I felt its firm grip around my trunk! And it was now quickly pulling me back up, up again, up from the bottom of that deep purple pit! But I got a quick look of Serpothel! Oh, such surprise on his ugly crawly face!

"What's happening? Am I being rescued? Oh, thank you, Maker!!!"

Serpothel's thundering cry reached us as we flew upward: "AAARRRGGGHHH!!!"

Then I felt them. There were six or so of them, these things which grabbed me and were now pulling me quickly upward. Yes, the climb was much quicker than the fall, and very soon I, or we, were swooshing upward through the pond's emptied opening, spraying purple and red flames everywhere!

Now, I saw who was left above. It was Stanamon and Snabeast, and both were running for cover, Stanamon racing to hide behind his pile of dead trees. And then we were done with that castle, even now swooshing through Stanamon's window! But how?! It was closed! But still, through it we flew, leaving that gray worm's castle behind!

"Yeah!!!" Was I happy!

5

ROLLING IN WOODCHIPS

We were flying through the clouds, white clouds in a blue sky. "I'm safe now. But who's carrying me? And where are we going?" I asked my-tree-self.

"To lands unknown," said the one carrying me through clouds and sky.

"You know my thoughts?" I thought.

"I know much more than that, precious tree."

I wondered what his greeting meant, but I asked, "What is your name?"

"Why do you ask my name?"

Our conversation was cut short. We were now gliding downward toward the earth below. The one carrying me gently settled us on the earth. I then turned to look at the one who rescued me from Serpothel and his flaming pit. I dropped flat on my face, unable to speak.

My rescuer was a sky-king, but He was the greatest of sky-kings! He was three times the size of any other! His leaves were all of white, of the whitest white! And the crown of His head and His two roots were all of gold, of the brightest shiniest gold! In fact, His crown and roots made the very best gold of Poor Orchard seem very much like the rolfed out berry bits of a little crown-flyer!

"Precious tree, you will find your answers as you walk toward your dreams, your second dream now walked. Put your trust in your Maker and fear not. See, you may speak now."

"But what of my family?"

"They are fine. Fear not."

Suddenly, great red flames approached, trees and grass disappearing into them. Before Great Sky-king covered me with his branches, I saw a strange thing. It looked like a giant tree of fire! It was spinning round and round! And it was coming near! It was then that Sky-king covered me. I could still feel some heat of the flames, but I was kept safe under his branches, untouched by that giant fiery tree. His branches soon lifted.

"What?! What was that?! The flames! A giant tree of fire?!"

"The flames of a dragon, an evil flying beast. It spit out a fiery twisting wind our way. He's gone for now. Precious Tree, trust in your Maker!"

Now with a great "SWOOSH!" of his branches, he was flying upward into the sky, golden flames trailing behind.

"Precious tree? How curious? That's what Great Sky-king calls me? I wonder what it means?"

I stood there for a bit, watching Sky-king fade away up into the clouds above.

I thought, "One dream walked, or more like dropped and flown, and two more to go? Oh, this is a lot of adventure for a walking tree. And that certainly is enough swooshing about for a walking tree for one day, I think. I'm tired."

I looked around to see where I was and where I had to be.

"Which way do I go now? Well, it looks like it's nearly morning. So I guess I'll just head toward that sunrise. Yes, I'll walk toward those mountains standing there before the sun."

Now midway through that day, the sun was standing high in the sky. And I was still making my way toward those distant mountains, toward the land of sunrises.

But I stopped. "What's that sound?"

I heard sounds of sadness, as if from a tree: "Oh... Oh... My poor wood. Poor me-tree. What am I to do?"

I thought, "It's coming from over there! Down below that cliff!"

After walking over to the cliff's edge, I looked down and saw him, a tree much like me, a walking tree, it seemed.

"Oh! You down there! What's wrong?! Do you need water?"

"Oh, my poor wood. Oh... No, it's not water I need. You see... I walked right off this cliff and am down here alone, now unable to get my-tree-self free. Oh, what's a tree to do?"

"Yes, I see... I'll try getting down there to help get you free!"

Well, getting over the cliff's edge was easy, but getting safely down there to this poor tree was still another matter. There were rocks, mud, and vines. But finally, I reached the poor tree.

"Well, what can I do? I can't see how to set you free. What's the problem? Is it your roots or your crown?"

"Oh, both roots and crown are stuck, it seems. Can you help me up?"

"Well, let me see..."

I first looked about. The crown was easier to free than were the roots. There was a rock on a branch here, one there. And then after a bit more work, his roots were freed as well.

"That's it! You did it! I'm free! Thank you!"

"Oh, I'm glad I could help. It was nothing, really."

"Oh! My name's Truly! What's yours?!"

"Truly? Wow! What a great name! My name's just Homer! But that's the name both my wife and our Maker like!"

"The Maker?"

"Oh, I'll tell you about that later."

"And you have a wife? Is she with you?"

"No, she's home with our son Ray. How about you? Are you here with family?"

"No, no family. Homer, are you from around here, or are you going somewhere?"

"Oh, I'm not from here. I'm walking toward the sunrise."

Truly said, "Oh! Me-tree too! Say, why don't we travel together since we're both walking toward the sunrise?"

I asked, "You're going that way too? But why?"

"Can't say just yet, but I'll tell you soon enough. How about you? Why are you going that way?"

"Well, Truly, as a sapling, I had three dreams, and I walked through all three. And these days, I again had three dreams. I've walked through only one, so far. So now, I'm walking toward the sunrise to find a wise, elder walking tree."

"But why, Homer?"

"Truly, I'm going to ask the elder the meaning of the two other dreams."

"How interesting! Homer, what are the last two dreams?"

"Well, Truly, we should be on our way, shouldn't we? Let's leave those dreams for another day."

"Yes, that's right. You know, Homer, our paths may be more alike than a common tree might think."

"Truly, you truly are a tree of mystery!

Truly laughed, "It didn't take you long for that one, did it, Homer?!"

I laughed back, "No, it didn't! Are you ready for walking, Friend?"

"Yes, I truly am. Ha! This way?" He was pointing several branches toward the land of sunrises.

I answered, "Yes! Let's follow the sunrise!"

"Follow the sunrise!"

We two trees walked several days from there, and we finally reached Sunrise Mountains. That's what I called them, because in the early morning they stood between us and the sunrise. Truly didn't seem to mind. Those mountains stretched so very far, both to the left and to the right. And so a climb up the middle of Sunrise Mountains seemed best.

I asked, "Are you ready to climb Sunrise Mountain to reach the sunrise?"

"Yes," said Truly. "That's the way to our sunrise. Let's get climbing."

There was no trail that we could see, and so the way was hard. And, of course, as the sun was falling to the earth behind us, it was getting even harder to find our way. We trees, as the reader must know, cannot see very well in the dark. So we usually leave the night to the four-rooters.

I finally said, "What do you say, Friend? Should we stop here for the night?"

"Yes, indeed," said Truly, being a tree of few words. And so we stopped there on Sunrise Mountain for the night.

Now the author has been in some noisy forests among both strange trees and walkers, but nothing could prepare me for the noise of that mountain night. There were the high shrieks of something like a dying hungry-runner and the low rumbling of a giant strange tree, either in great mumblings or in great falling to the earth. And there were all those bursts of sound between the shrieks and the rumblings. I thanked our Maker that night that He didn't make we trees to be things that sleep. How could anything sleep in the night on that mountain?

But suddenly, I could no longer hear the noise of that night. You see, my seeing knots were keeping me too busy now with something before me. They were seeing a frightful thing walking in the night. I pointed my crown toward that thing approaching and said, "Truly, what is that? Do you believe in ghosts?"

Truly answered, "I've heard of them but never saw one."

I whispered, "Ignore it."

"Okay," whispered Truly.

The ghostly walker was much closer than we had thought. It looked to be a tree-ghost still some ways away, but if it was, in fact, a much smaller ghost, it was very near indeed. It was so close, in fact, that it could hear what we trees were whispering. And that we did not expect.

"What are we ignoring?" came the whisper from the walking ghost.

Truly and I didn't say a word. We had both agreed to ignore the ghost, and that was exactly what we did. Only silence was found among we two trees. You see, trees don't like ghosts. And this walker was truly a real ghost, a strange, glowing blur under the moonlight. It was the first real ghost I had ever seen.

"Woodpecker got your tongue?" were the unwelcomed words from the little ghost.

As it came closer, we trees could see this unwelcomed ghost much better. It wasn't a tree ghost at all! It was a bush ghost! Of course, a bush ghost in the moonlight can easily be taken to be a tree ghost. Ask any tree.

I was still shaking a bit with fear, and Truly was keeping quiet, so I just had to say, "Oh, you're a bush ghost."

"Well, I'm neither ghost nor bush, Friend. Yes, you could call me a bush if you like, but we brambles call our-bramble-selves brambles."

I said, "You're a bramble?"

"Yes, you see these blackberries? I'm a fairly common bramble in some places. Now what's this talk of ghosts?"

"Oh, nothing really," I laughed.

I heard Truly laughing a little too.

Correcting myself, I said, "A bramble, huh? Yes, I've seen a few brambles, but a walking bramble I've never met. How is it, little bramble, that you walk about as we trees do?"

The bramble answered, "How would you trees answer that question when asked? How is it that you trees walk as a bramble does?"

We were all now in a very awkward place, both bramble and tree, each a stranger to the other, each questioning the other how he could walk as oneself did. We three stood there in the moonlit night of that thunderous, shrieking Sunrise Mountain, just looking at the other, after asking the other the same question and yet getting no answer.

"Yes," I thought. "This must be a popular question among walking trees and walking brambles. We all seem to be asking it."

I decided to be the first to show how friendly a walking tree really is.

"Oh... I'm Homer, and this is my friend, Truly. And, as you can see, we two trees are of the common walking kind. And who, may I ask, are you?"

"As I said, I'm a blackberry bramble, and I'm of the common walking kind my-bramble-self. And you can call me Stickler, because that's my name, but why it is, I cannot say. For I am just a common blackberry bramble, after all."

I said, "Glad to meet you, Stickler."

"Glad to meet you," offered Truly.

"Pleased to meet you two walking trees, I'm sure," as Stickler reached out a stickly branch to us, neither of us knowing why.

"Oh!" I blurted. "What's the meaning of your extended stickly branch?"

"Oh, trees don't know? With a branch, we brambles very nearly make contact with each other. In this way, we show our friendliness. Of course, we brambles don't mean for our branches to make contact, though it does happen sometimes. It happened to some bramble friends of mine while saying 'Hello'. Oh, it can ruin a bramble's day, trying to figure out how to get free from the branch of another."

"Yes," I said. "I can see that. It must be a problem for brambles. We trees don't have such a custom, but I guess we trees could without much trouble."

Truly nodded in agreement.

"I see," said Stickler. "Well, where are you two off to? You don't live on this mountain, do you?"

Truly was shaking his crown "no". And I was sure that he wasn't going to add any words to that, so I began answering this strange, walking bramble my-tree-self.

"Well, I recently had three tree dreams, with number two dream already walked. And now I'm on my way toward the land of sunrises to find a wise elder tree who can explain to me my other two dreams."

"Oh, I see," said the little bramble. "And what of your friend?" The little bramble now seemed to turn toward Truly: "Truly, what about you?"

"Cannot say just yet, little bramble."

"Truly is truly a mystery," I said. "Both to you, little bramble, and to me-tree."

Truly just ignored us. Those were the last of Truly's words that night.

"Oh, I see..." mumbled the bramble.

"And what of you?" I asked. "Do you live on this mountain?"

"No."

And that was the end of the little bramble's words that night. We three just stood there on that moonlit Sunrise Mountain, passing the night in silence. We stood there among the shrieks and gasps of fear of little ones and the thunderings of giants, who were either mumbling or falling, with every unwelcomed, curious sound in between, from the groans of small somethings passing away to the "thud, thud, thudding" of big somethings passing by. This moonlit night was very much alive with the sounds of a great mountain. But silence still ruled among we three, we two trees and a little bramble.

Though we trees never sleep, the morning comes along soon enough. Along with the rising of the sun, I could see both my friend Truly and the little bramble nearby.

I spoke up. "I'm off to find the meanings of my last two dreams, out there toward the rising sun. I'll be going now while it's still rising. See you later, perhaps."

Truly answered as I had expected: "I too am off to the land of rising suns. Let's be off then. Farewell, little bramble!"

But the little bramble's answer surprised us. "I'm also walking into the sunrise. Let's go together then, shall we?"

I quickly thought of some excuses, of course. "Oh, you needn't do that, little bramble! We trees walk rather fast! Don't we, Truly?!"

"Yes, we trees certainly do. No, you needn't do that, little bramble."

"Oh... I see that you two trees have never journeyed with a bramble, and a blackberry bramble at that! Don't you worry! I'll slow down enough for you! Otherwise, I'm sure you could never keep up with a blackberry bramble!"

Well, it was settled then. We three, two trees and a little bramble, were to walk together toward the sunrise. Of course, Truly and I tried to show the little bramble how useless it was to keep up with us trees, but surprisingly, that little bramble took the lead, leaving us in the dust. And even when we trees turned more to the left or to the right, the little bramble somehow kept his lead just ahead us. It really was useless trying to lose that little bramble. We trees quickly learned that.

Strangely though, as we were walking along our way with the sun quite high, my two travel partners each took off on their own ways, one going this way and the other that, Truly first and then little bramble.

I thought to my-tree-self, "Oh, what kind of travel partners are these? How strange they are!"

But surprisingly, later sometime they each found me as I was strolling on my way. I was just heading toward the middle of two taller mountains, between the two that held the sunrise that morning. But my two walking partners were still curiously silent, both when returning and even while walking. "How strange, this tree and bramble!" I thought. But I tried hard to keep my thoughts quietly to my-tree-self.

That second night with the little bramble came sooner than I had expected.

"Oh! Truly! Little bramble! What say you two to stopping here for the night?"

They were both so curiously silent, but stop there for the night we did. My tree thought was, "Oh, why do we still travel together if not together at all?" Well, you can be sure that was my-tree thought by that second night all right.

Soon, the sun was rising as it did that first morning with the little bramble. And again, there was only silence while walking. "Oh, how alone a tree can be when journeying together with such a strange tree and an even stranger bramble!" I quietly thought.

And, yes, that same loneliness after walking together a while on that first day happened again on this second day. When the sun was high, Truly turned off this way and the little bramble that way.

But we trees make the best of our days, and today was no different. I was walking along just fine, that is, until they appeared. No, it wasn't that strange Truly and that even stranger bramble. I need to explain.

I didn't know their language. It must have been some woodsmen language, for these certainly looked like the woodsmen I had been warned about in Rich Orchard. They walked on two roots and carried something that must have been an axe, something quite sharp and partly made of wood. Oh, I shiver again thinking of our meeting on that day.

There were three of them taking their turns with me-tree, each with its two walking roots and two waving branches, with which they swung their axes. And oh, how they swung them! They swung them right through me, and they seemed to be laughing about it. Oh! Those cruel woodsmen with their axes!

"Ooowwweee! Oww! Oww! Oww!" I shouted at the top of my branches. At first, of course, I felt the pain from their axes. But soon the pain just disappeared, but no, not the woodsmen! They didn't disappear!

So they went to work swinging at me, this poor tree. Oh, how I wished they would just stop after a few swings. But, no, they didn't stop! Off came my roots, first one by one, then two by two and next, by threes. Off they all came. "Oh, my walking days are over!" I mourned.

And, oh no! My clear, living sap began to run about on the rocks! I thought quite loudly, "What will become of me-tree, the tree?!!!"

And no, they didn't stop with just my roots. Next, they swung about at my crown, oh, my wonderful, green crown. My long, swinging branches were quickly chopped off and thrown about! Not one branch was left! Not even one! "Oh, what more can they do to me?! Nothing more, can they?! Surely, they can do me-tree no more harm?!"

You see, I wasn't thinking clearly at that time. There was more, it seems, to be done to my tree life. Both my roots and crown were gone. So they then began to swing about at my trunk, my brown trunk that was all that I had left to call "me"!

You see, I could no longer even call me Me-tree! I knew my tree days were nearly over.

I shouted out my thoughts, "Oh no!!!" But why did I wait so long? I finally remembered to cry out to my Maker. "Oh, Maker, my Maker! Oh, please help me, whatever is left of me! May these woodsmen stop! Please save my life, whatever is left of it!!!"

But it was soon over. I was over, done. All was lost. What was once a tree, even a walking tree with a wonderful crown, quick walking roots, and a healthy trunk, was now mere wood chips on the rocks. I was no longer the walking tree.

I, or, that is, my seeing and speaking part, was now just rolling about like a piece of fruit. That was all that was left of me the tree. I asked my-something-self, "Homer, what are you now? Are you even a tree, or are you a rolling something? Homer, all you have left is your seeing and speaking part of your once-wonderful-tree-self."

Then I asked my-something-self, "Now what did Sky-ranger call this part that's left of me? What was it? Hmmm…"

The reader may understand that I had a hard time thinking after losing most all of my-tree-self. I asked again, "What would she say I am now? I got it! A head! She would call me a head now! That's it!"

I don't know why I felt so happy to remember this at that time. But somehow it made me feel better to know what I was or wasn't now.

I figured out that me-tree, the walking tree, was now me-head, the rolling head. But my happy feelings soon left. I could now see that I was able to do nothing more than roll about on my woodchips. Oh, how down I felt, so lost and hopeless. Would any tree in a similar situation feel differently?

"This is bad, so very bad! It can't get any worse than this!" thought I, a tree head rolling in woodchips.

6

SOMETHING UNEXPECTED

I was down, so very down, even really down on the ground, this rolling head of a tree. But to make matters worse, and, yes, that was possible after all, the woodsmen had a playful four-root runner. Oh! It made this strange, loud sound like "Wuff!!! Wuff!!!" And I did not like this four-root runner, no, not at all.

And I liked it even less when it picked me up with its disappearing opening with all its white disappearing branches, letting its slimy, yellow sap cover me, this rolling head of a tree. It picked me up and tossed me about the earth, as if I were a funny thing.

"Oh, my Maker, how long will this be?"

I looked about where I had to, that is, wherever the four-root runner wished to point my seeing knots. You see, I was unable to turn this way or that on my own, having neither trunk nor roots. I called out, "Oh, my Maker, I will trust in you. What else can I do?"

I tried shouting at this playful four-root runner, but I soon found that nothing I did would help. For one thing, hardly any sound came out from my head. And for another thing, it seemed that when my speaking opening was moving about, it only gave the four-root runner more fun with me, this rolling tree head. It tossed me about even more, with its "Wuff!!! Wuff!!!" and the shaking of its end root. By now I just kept my speech opening shut and waited for all this to end somehow.

"It must end," I thought. "But how," I wondered, or that is, my head wondered. "How will all this end for me, this rolling head?" It was certainly, by now, a hopeless situation for a walking tree. You see, I was surely, by now, becoming a realist, and that, just before my end. I knew now that I was in really great trouble.

My thoughts continued a while longer anyway, "I may be only a head, but at least I know I am only a head. That does mean something, doesn't it? Isn't that one good thing?" And I thought it must be, though I was having a hard time thinking, of course.

And then another thought came to me, this rolling tree head: "This seems familiar. Have I been here before? But when?! Where?! Oh yes!!!" My rolling head thoughts continued, "I felt this way when I was just a seed! Okay, I know this, but what good will it do me now!?"

Well, that playful four-rooter did finally try to disappear me, or my head that is, as all four-rooters probably do. But unable to disappear my head, it finally tossed it about just a little too far. "I'm free!" I shouted to my-head-self. "At least what's left of my head is free!"

You see, it lost my head when it started rolling down the hill toward the cliff. I knew a cliff was coming. At every turn of my head, there it was, the cliff just ahead of me.

And then off my head went, flying in the wind with nothing but sky all around, and my poor, flying head now thought, "Who am I? What am I? Am I still Homer? Or am I merely Homer's head? What now? How long can a tree head fly, flying like the crown-flyers of the sky? I have no crown with which to fly. So it looks like I'm only flying downward... Down to where? And to what? To another four-rooter? To more woodsmen? Oh, why did I ever leave my family and friends? Because of my dreams? Did I have to??? Here I am dropping from the sky, but for how long? There! I see dark clouds ahead. Or are they clouds?"

"SPLASH!!!"

Finally, I, or that is, my head, dropped into very deep waters. I never hit the bottom! I just dropped that one time, down deep into the waters, and then I flew upward again toward the sky! I thought I would fly right up into the sky forever, but I soon found my-head-self dropping again like a rock into the waters. And they were such fast-running waters!

After some time, I asked my-tree-head-self, "Will this water never stop?" Oh, it seemed days that I was going up and down, up and down, in that fast, moving water, hitting rocks along the way now and then. I thought, "How long must my tree head follow these waters? And to where? Will I even like it when I get there? Oh… don't I have, or my tree head has, another dream to walk or roll through? Isn't that creepy-crawly dream still left?"

Suddenly, the waters stopped, and I thought, "Where am I now?" I soon found out. I was in a great sky of waters! So much water everywhere! "Where could this be?! Oh! I'm in the world of water-flyers! So many! But they belong here! I don't belong here! Oh, no! A big water-flyer's coming my way, its disappearing opening is opening wider and wider!"

I shouted, "Oh! Big water-flyer, don't! Don't disappear me, my tree head! It's all that I have left…"

"Chomp! Gurgle-gurgle-gurgle… Glump!"

"Homer's head, so this is what a big water-flyer is like inside! It's so... so dark. What is a tree, or a tree head, to do? Think Homer... Think Homer's tree head... What to do? Anything?" After some time... my tree head got a good idea: "That's it! Our Planter!"

I looked up the best I could from inside the water-flyer's darkness, trying to look up past the sky, which must have been up there somewhere still, and I spoke, "Oh, my Planter, You who planted me in a forest of strange trees, You who led my roots to others of my kind, some good and others bad, You who gave me-tree, when I was still me-tree, the hill of my dreams and the family I could never have dreamt of, You who, I think, bears with silly trees like me-tree, now me-head, just a tree head of Homer, under the waters in the darkness of a big water flyer, my searching for my dreams leading me here to this... Oh, our Maker! Please may I yet live and leave this place of darkness. May I somehow be a tree again... I believe all things are possible for You! I will thank my Maker. I trust in You."

"Glump, glump! Gurgling-gurgling-gurgling! Swoosh, kapush! RRRoooooooolllfff!!!"

Praise our Maker! I now found my-tree-head-self flying upward to the waters' crown! Again, I could see the sky, there above the churning waters, the big water-flyer now saying "Goodbye" with a great splash of its giant end branch, only to disappear again into the deep waters, crown-flyers flying about, trying to avoid that great splash.

"Where... where am I? Oh, I see the earth again. I see it coming near."

My tree head hit the rocks, the waves finally pushing it up above most of them. And there I was, or there my tree head was, sitting there on a pile of rocks, looking up at the sky and its sunshine. Looking upward beyond the sky: "Oh, thank you, our Maker, my Planter!!! Thank you!!! But what is next?"

Now out of the corner of my seeing knot, I could see a big, dead water-flyer. It was floating along on the waters, and it was slowly coming my way. It finally got washed right up onto the rocks by the waves. It was now covering me, blocking out the warm rays of the sun.

So again, I was in darkness, and again, it was a big water-flyer. I really tried to cheer my-head-self up. I offered, "At least I'm just under it and not in it this time." My tree head lay there on those rocks for some time, held there by the rotting trunk of a dead water-flyer.

You know, my tree-sense kept telling me that things could never get worse than they were. But now I finally saw that my tree-sense was not making much sense at all. In fact, I even saw Hope walking away, leaving my tree head here under this hopeless mess. I thought, "She's looking for another tree. Homer's head, she doesn't want to waste any more time here with you."

But then there came a more stubborn thought, "Grandad! What did Grandad tell me when I was just a little sapling? What was it?"

My thoughts carried me off and away from my slimy mess into the distant past. I was that little sapling listening to Grandaddy.

"Better a live stump than a dead giant, Grandson."

"Grandaddy, what does that mean?" I needed an answer. I knew I needed it now. But Grandad was drifting off, away from my thoughts. I could hardly see him now.

"Oh, my Maker! What did Grandad mean?! I can't remember!"

Again, that little sapling asked, "Grandaddy, what does that mean?"

"Grandson, look over there at that poor stump. Now, look at his poor giant neighbor. Grandson, which one is living?"

"Grandaddy, the stump is living. Red's stump is still alive."

"That's right, Grandson. And Red's giant neighbor, Skytree, stands nearby, reaching up into the sky. But Skytree is dead. Grandson, better a live stump than a dead giant."

"Grandaddy, but what does that mean?"

"Grandson, the living have Hope."

My thoughts carried me back again to my poor tree head under a rotting water-flyer. I repeated Grandad's words, "The living have Hope."

I asked my-head-self, "Homer's head, are you living?" And I heard what I asked, and so I knew how to answer: "Yes!" I added, "Homer's head, you have Hope!"

I now saw Hope stop, turn around, and look at me! She came over and was looking for me under my smelly mess! She found me! I shouted, "Hope returned!!!" And then something began happening, something very familiar...

"Am I... Is my tree head... a seedling?! Again?! Really?! Thank you, Maker!!!"

I had roots. And I could feel them growing. Soon they were pulling me out from under my rotting mess. They were taking me up higher onto the earth, finally making me-seedling settle down among green grasses of the earth. These grasses seemed to be waving at me-seedling. I had roots! I was a seedling!

And there I sat for some time, just waiting... But it was worth the wait. Sooner than later, I had my old self back – roots, trunk, and crown - all of me back together again, but better than before! So, actually, I was my new self now. I was young again. Only my head still seemed a bit old. But that was surely nothing to complain about, was it?

You see, if my tree head were new too, wouldn't that mean that I was then another tree? Wouldn't my tree tale have to stop about here, with a new beginning? Oh, that would put both me and my readers in such an uncomfortable situation indeed! Fortunately for us all, we can just continue with this, my original tree's tale. And for this, I am very happy.

I again was a walking tree, and so I went about walking. I went out exploring this new earth. You see, after some time of looking about, it was clear that this was not my old earth where I had grown up from seed through sapling to tree.

And I found that there were no trees here on my new earth, and so, certainly, there were no walking trees like my-new-tree-self. My family wasn't here on this smaller, new earth either. So I asked my-tree-self, "Why am I here?"

That cruel word "mistake," which I had hardly ever heard or used, seemed very real to me here on this new earth. I thought, "So this is what a mistake is? I shouldn't be here? I think this must be a very big mistake. Why else would I be here?" You see, I could see no other reason.

My only friends here on this new earth were the flyers of the waters, who I could barely see unless they left the water dead, and the flyers of the sky, who would merely pass me by without a crown-flyer thought, it seemed. These were my only friends on my new earth. So, yes, I felt alone.

The time alone here gave me nothing to do and nowhere to go except into some tree thoughts. And so I thought and thought and finally called out to my Planter: "Oh Planter, you made me new, a young walking tree again, here in this new earth. But what am I to do now? Am I to fly, to fly the waters or sky? I think that is surely beyond me. After all, I'm only a tree. Oh Planter, please help me. Please free me from this new earth. May I again be home with my family."

And it was then that I saw it, a pile of broken trees on the sand near the waters. "Why hadn't I seen this before," I thought. "What could this mean?"

And then I said to my-tree-self, "Hey! My head was rolling about and then flying through sky and waters to get here, to a pile of dead trees?! Then isn't this my first dream? It must be!!!"

Then I thought that maybe because I went through such a very difficult time, losing everything but my tree head, and nearly losing that, that I just hadn't been thinking in my right mind.

You see, I hadn't thought of this as my first dream, till now. (Ha! I wonder how many readers saw this before me!) So, I finally saw that all these recent crazy things happening to me were about my first dream. Now I knew this, or at least, I was now pretty sure of it.

Then I thought, "How did these broken trees end up here, all lying about dead?" Soon my wondering was over. For I saw it, a two-rooter, a small one, smaller than those woodsmen who cut me-tree up into me-head.

It was calling out something like, "Help! Help!" That is what I finally guessed it was shouting.

Then I thought a bit too loudly, "But what can I do?"

"How can you, a tree, talk?"

"Well, yes, we trees usually don't..."

Then it said, "And how did you get here? You weren't here a moment ago."

"Well, yes, I just walked over here when I saw all these dead trees, you see..."

"Dead trees? You mean my boat? Oh, I really shouldn't talk right now, you see..."

Yes, I could see. It was stuck under some dead trees, and only its two walking roots and a bit of its crown could be seen. It looked very uncomfortable to me, but what does a tree know about such things as two-rooters under a pile of dead trees and its comfort?

So I asked, "Are you, little two-rooter, comfortable?"

"Two-rooter? Comfortable? No... You see, tree, I'm stuck under my boat, and I can't get myself free. I need help."

"You need help? Say, you aren't... you aren't... a woodsman, are you, by any chance?"

"A woodsman? No, of course I'm not! I'm a girl!"

I thought, "A girl? Well, I guess since it's not a woodsman..." It was later after she was freed that she explained some of her words, like "girl," to me.

"Oh, I see," I said. "Then if you're not a woodsman, I suppose I could help. But I don't know if I can do any good. That pile of dead trees is a very big pile indeed. I don't think even five walking trees could move that... that..."

"Boat."

"Oh, 'boat'. But I'll try."

To my surprise, I lifted that pile of dead trees right up and off the little two-rooter. I guessed my new tree parts, that is, my new roots, trunk, and crown, most of me, must have come with more tree power than my old tree parts had before the axing by those woodsmen.

"Oh! There! That's it, isn't it? Are you free now?"

"Yes! Oh, Tree! I lost all hope! Baaawaaa! Baaawaaa! Baaa..."

The poor, freed little two-rooter was now raining sap out her seeing knots. Oh, what a downpour it was! I worried so, thinking that it might dry up soon. And so I said, "Little one, be careful with raining all your sap away. You might just dry up. You know, it does happen sometimes."

"Raining all my sap away? Oh... I... I... think I understand what you're saying, friendly tree. Oh... Tree... I lost hope! Baaawaaa! Baaa..."

"Oh but, little one, you have found her now. You have Hope again. She has returned!"

"Oh, Tree, I'm sorry... I had lost all and was stuck under this boat for a long time and thought I would never again have hope."

I could then honestly tell the little two-rooter, "I understand. Yes, little one, I understand. But are you comfortable now?"

"Yes, thank you, I am. Thank you, my talking and walking tree friend for saving me. Oh, what's your name?"

"Oh, any tree would do the same... My name... Well, I've never talked with any two-rooters besides those really bad woodsmen that cut me to pieces, so I've never ever given my name to a two-rooter. But I guess since you are a small two-rooter and you seem nice enough and you're not a woodsman, as you say, I guess I could tell you my name. My name was Me-tree, and still might be when I speak of my-tree-self, but now most trees just call me Homer. I think that's my name because when I'm not there, I always dream of walking home. And, may I ask, what is your name, little two-rooter?"

"The woodsmen cut you to pieces?! Oh, my!!! I'm so sorry to hear that!!!"

"Well, I'm doing much better now... Really."

"Yes, I can see that! Well, my name is Jill. Me-tree but now Homer, do you live here?"

"Oh, no. I just ended up here after losing everything but my head, which then rolled all about on my woodchips because of a playful four-rooter, finally rolling off the cliff and flying through sky and waters, ending up in a big water-flyer only to get covered over by another dead one, and ..."

"Oh, my!" the little two-rooter Jill said. "You really must teach me your language! You see, I don't speak or understand tree language very well. And I'm sure I don't understand what you're saying. Because if I did understand, then you were rolling and flying about as only a tree head! And I know that can't be right!"

"Oh, okay... Jill, do you live here?"

"Oh, no. I was just out for a little fun in the old sailboat when some huge waves drove me toward those boulders over there, which wrecked our boat, and then the waves drove me up onto the beach here, leaving me trapped under this old boat, and..."

"Oh, my... I don't understand two-rooter words very well. Maybe we, a two-rooter and a tree, can discuss our strange words sometime later?"

"Well, yes, of course. Oh, Me-tree, I mean Homer, do you have any food?"

"Food? What is food? Is it dangerous like...
an axe?!"

"Oh, no! Not dangerous at all! That's right!
Homer, you're a tree! Trees don't eat food! I guess
you don't know this, but we humans eat food to
stay strong and healthy."

"I see... The woodsmen were strong and
probably very healthy. Well, you'll have to teach me
some of these words, too. Maybe we can walk
around my new earth and see if there's any of that
foot you're looking for?"

"Oh, funny tree! Not foot! Food! Ha, ha, ha!"

Jill, the nice little woodsman, was laughing,
and so I thought I would begin laughing too. "Ha,
ha!" I still didn't know much about Jill, after all.

We two, she with two roots and me with
many, did some looking around, and I think we
found something like she was looking for. She
called it food. But there wasn't very much of it there
on that new earth, and so we two made a plan to
return to my old earth, where there was probably
more of that food she wanted.

We gathered together those poor dead trees that she called a boat, and with her on the dead trees and me on my own, being a tree my-tree-self, we two went out into the waters.

My best guess was that we should fly through the waters toward the mountains in the distance, but soon the waters were pulling Jill further away from those mountains. So I did my best to help. I was able to hold on to Jill's dead trees while flying through the waters with my other roots, flying slowly but surely toward the mountains and away from the new earth. And yes, we finally reached the old earth where the mountains stood waiting.

We sat on the rocks awhile. Jill said, "Oh, Homer, you saved my life again! Thank you, my friend, my tree friend!"

I still didn't know exactly how to answer a little two-rooter that called herself a girl but looked a lot like the woodsmen who swung their axes at me, that is, all about my head, but I did guess that I could say something like "Happy to help, Jill."

"You know, Homer... how funny that you have a cross on your face! You know, it must mean something!"

"Cross on my face? It's funny?"

"No, not really funny... Homer, it's coming back to me now. When I was little, I was with my parents, and I think we came here, though we weren't supposed to visit this island. And we three saw three walking palm trees on a hill. Yes, I think it was on this island. The trees didn't have many branches, and, of course, that's why they looked like three crosses."

"Palm trees... crosses? Jill, what are crosses?"

"Well, they looked like three crosses. The middle one was the important one, of course. That's because the middle one was where..."

"Sweetie!!!"

"Jill!!!"

Well, our conversation was suddenly cut short. After learning about crosses, I was going to ask Jill to join me on my journey to the sunrises in order to find a wise tree elder to ask about my one remaining dream. And I thought that maybe he could help Jill, too... help her get back home.

But before we could talk about crosses and the tree elder and home, another pile of dead trees came our way, and it even had two more two-rooters on it that looked very much like woodsmen. But surprisingly, they also looked very much like the two bigger two-rooters of the three that visited Dream Hill. It was only later that another two-rooter friend confirmed this and explained more about their visit to Dream Hill.

I would have had a good talk with Jill, but I suddenly found my-tree-self becoming way too shy to speak around the two bigger two-rooters. So I just held my thoughts and words and said nothing more. Yes, I felt sorry to Jill, but what could I do? Trees just don't talk to strangers, especially to strangers that look too much like woodsmen.

Well, this is something like what I heard from Jill and her parents:

"Jill! Is that you?!"

"Dad! Mom! You found me!"

"Jill! We were so worried about you! How could you take the old boat out like that?! We were so worried!"

"Sorry, Dad, Mom. I was just going out for a little bit, but the sea pulled me away."

"Are you okay, Honey? Are you hurt? Oh, look at you! You hit your head!"

"Yes, Mom. I'm okay. Hey! Mom, Dad, meet my tree friend, Homer! Homer, these are my parents!"

"This is your tree friend? Oh, Kiddo, you hurt yourself all right. Oh... Let's get you to a doctor!"

"Dad, I'm okay, really. Thanks to Homer! You see, Homer saved me! Homer, tell my mom and dad how you rescued me, twice!"

Oh, how sorry I felt to Jill, but trees just don't easily talk to strangers. I hoped she would understand. I couldn't even say "good-bye" to her.

"Homer? Me-tree? My friend?"

"Come on, Honey. Come on into the boat. We'll get you taken care of. Yes, come on. Let's get you to the doctor!"

"Bye, Homer! Bye, my tree friend! I understand! I do! Thank you, Homer!!!"

Yes, I did wave a branch a bit as she left. She was a friend, after all. I watched as their pile of dead trees flew them away through the deep waters. But after a bit, a little sap in my seeing knots made it a little hard to see.

"Farewell, Jill, you who fly through great waters on piles of poor, dead trees. Farewell, little friend."

And I thought, "Well, I'm back on my old earth again. Now to find that wise elder tree, before getting back home to Eve and Ray. Yes! I'm walking home soon! I just need the meaning of one more dream! Yeah!"

I didn't know exactly where I was, but I thought I could just wait through the night, and in the morning, I would again be on my way toward the sunrises.

The next morning, I was again heading into the sunrise, but this time I was alone. I thought, "Being alone is better than walking with a secretive tree and a strange bramble of few words. But I might miss my new friend Jill. She talked some, and I don't think she was a woodsman. Also, her mother and father didn't seem to carry an axe. They all seemed friendly enough to me-tree."

7

HOW TO FRY A DRAGON

I might mention here that I have heard that non-trees don't think out loud like trees generally do. This is why a tree must be very careful not to think around strangers, especially the two and four-rooter kinds. And that is why non-trees think that trees can't talk. Trees are very careful about who they think around.

And, of course, on this early, sunny morning while stepping toward the rising sun, there were no listeners about that I could see. I might also mention here that, unlike trees, brambles don't think out loud. At least, I never heard the little bramble think.

When the sun was high, I was walking toward a big mountain where I saw the sun rise that morning. I, fortunately, hadn't been doing much thinking; for, surprisingly, both Truly and the little bramble were standing nearby!

"Truly, what a surprise! What happened to you, my friend! Did you see the woodsmen?! They cut me to pieces, you know..."

"They did! Oh... they did? Hello, Homer! They cut you to pieces?! But look at you! You look like a young, healthy tree! Is that really you?! But I know it is! You've got that tree thing on your face! Are you... Are you... Homer's ghost?!"

"No. It's me... I'm Homer! I'm no ghost! You see, our Maker did this for me after I was disappeared by a big water-flyer and then covered by another dead one, and then..."

"What?! Give thanks to your Maker! I'm so happy to see you, Homer! And, no, I didn't see any woodsmen. You... you just disappeared! But this strange, little bramble here... well, it hasn't left me alone for all these many moons!"

It was time now to say "hello" to the little bramble, which we trees could not seem to lose.

"Oh, little bramble, you're here! Hello!"

You see, we walking trees are a very polite kind of tree.

"Hello, Homer! Welcome back to the living! And I knew you'd be heading toward the sunrise soon!"

"You did?" said both of us trees at the same time.

But then I had to ask, "Little bramble, how did you know?"

"Oh, a little bird told me."

I asked, "Was it Sky-ranger?"

But the little bramble just turned and walked toward the great mountain before us. After we three had walked some ways, he looked my way (I'm guessing he did. For a bramble's face is certainly hard to see.) and whispered, "Truly talked with the woodsmen."

I thought Truly must have heard the little bramble, but perhaps he didn't. After stopping for a moment, Truly again walked along with us toward the mountain. But, of course, I wondered very quietly at this time, "Who is telling the truth, Truly or the little bramble?" Now we three were once again walking along in silence.

We reached Sunrise Mountain that same day before the sun went down. I called it Sunrise Mountain, though it may have been a different mountain from the first. If it was the same mountain, we were certainly standing on a different root.

I still don't know what was beyond that mountain, but there was no need to know; for there at the root of that mountain, I found what I was looking for all these many moons. There before us was an orchard of walking trees. And all the trees were gathered around an older one. I thought, "Is this the wise elder I've been looking for? Can he help me?"

The elder tree that all the trees were standing around looked much like most other walking trees. He had that flattened crown, brown trunk, and the walking roots. But his crown wasn't all green. There was some orange here and there. I wondered if the orange color came with age. I have seen some older walking trees with somewhat faded crowns. Also, his trunk was rather fat, but I would never tell him that. I waited until their meeting was over to talk with him, just as the sun was going down.

"Hello. I'm Homer. And I have come from far away to talk with you. May I call you 'Teacher', as others do?"

"Yes, please do. You came here to talk with me? What did you wish to talk about?"

"Teacher, I had three dreams many moons ago. And I was planning to ask you their meanings. But I've walked through two dreams already, and so I'm here to ask of the third. I wonder if you would be so kind to tell me its meaning."

"Three dreams? Okay... Please tell me all three."

"Well, in the first one, I was rolling all about and then flying through sky and waters to help someone I did not know. And this dream, Teacher, I understand, for I did roll about and fly through sky and waters, finally helping one I did not know."

"I see... And the second?"

"The second dream was of ugly beasts with four-rooter crowns and two-rooter trunks, each followed by me, all of us falling through purple fire. But next, it was me alone, flying through white clouds. And this dream, I have also walked through."

"Oh, I see... Very interesting. Yes... And the third?"

"Yes, this dream hasn't happened yet. I was standing in an orchard of walking trees. And we were all listening to an old tree as it talked and talked and talked. And, suddenly, the old tree's crown fell to the earth and burst into flames! And then I saw it! An earth-crawler's ugly crown was sticking out from the tree trunk! You know, it was one of those earth-crawlers that have no walking roots and no branches, the kind that is always

sticking out a thin red tongue while saying,
'Ssss...'".

"I see...," said Teacher. "And next? What...
what happened next?"

"As I was watching this crawler still trying to
hide in the tree, it suddenly burst into flames! The
ugly crawler was dead, and it was burning up!"

"Oh!!!"

"But next, I had the strangest thought: 'Will
they kill me?' Teacher, please tell me the meaning
of this dream. It's been like a giant tree leaning on
me all this time. Can you help me, please?"

"Isss... is that all?"

"Yes, Teacher."

"Thank you, Homer, for telling me your
dreams. I'm sure there's a meaning for this third
one, too. You did say... the first two happened?"

"Yes, Teacher, I walked through both
dreams."

"Hmmm... I'll think this over, and we'll talk
again tomorrow. But don't speak of your dreams to
any tree, not until you and I speak again."

"Yes, I understand, Teacher. I look forward to hearing your wisdom. Good rest."

"Yesss... good rest."

But before I could turn, Teacher strongly stepped on my roots.

"Aaauuuggghhh!"

Teacher whispered, "What's wrong?"

I whispered back, "Teacher, that hurt."

"Oh, don't be silly. Sssee you in the morning."

"Yes, Teacher."

But it did hurt, and I very quietly wondered, "Why did he do that?"

That night, I found a quiet spot to rest. But how strange! I couldn't see Truly or the little bramble anywhere. I wondered where they could be.

Morning came with the rising sun, and I then saw Truly nearby.

"Good walking, Truly."

"Yes, good walking, Homer. I have something to tell you."

"What is it, Friend?"

Truly whispered, "The little bramble... He left the orchard yesterday when you went to talk to Teacher. And I followed him, careful not to be seen."

"Yes... What happened?"

"After some walking from here, the little bramble found a quiet, lonely spot and had a meeting. Homer, the bramble talked with an earth-crawler! You know, the kind with no roots or branches! Homer, they're friends! They were talking and laughing! Homer, what do you think?!"

"Friends with an earth-crawler? That can't be good. Truly, be careful. That little bramble is our enemy. I thought so... Be careful."

"Yes, Friend. And you, too, be careful. Beware the bramble!"

Our much-needed talk ended, and the sun was now warm. So all we trees began gathering around Teacher.

"What wise words will he speak today? Can he help me?" I wondered.

I might mention here that I did not hear a word of the teacher's message the day before. I was

so busy thinking about my dreams, especially the
third one. And, of course, I had to keep some
distance from the orchard in order to keep my
thoughts to my-tree-self. "Today," I thought. "I'll
listen to Teacher's words of wisdom. Yes, I will. I'm
pretty sure he'll help me with the meaning of my
last dream. No, I'm sure he will. I have a good
feeling about Teacher."

So this is how the lesson went:

"Guards! That new tree over there! Hold
him! Don't let him leave!"

"Yes, Teacher!"

And with that, our lesson started, with me
being held as a bad tree by the two guards.

"What?" I asked my-tree-self. "What's
happening here? I guess I should've paid attention
to yesterday's lesson." I looked toward the teacher:
"Teacher, what happened?!"

"Silence! Guards, keep that evil tree quiet!"

"Yes, Teacher!"

I turned toward the guards and questioned,
"What's wrong?! Why am I in trouble?!"

"Quiet, evil tree! You know why!"

But, no, I really didn't.

I very quietly thought to my-tree-self, "Maybe I shouldn't have told Teacher about my dreams."

Teacher now began today's lesson. "Think Orchard! Gather around now! It is so sad that your first teacher died recently. So sad... But it is good that I am here to guide you thinking trees into your best possible tree life. So let me give you something more to think about today. After all, that is why we are all here today in this early morning, here in the fog below this mountain. We are all here for very important thinking. Is that not right?"

All thinking trees shouted, "Yes!!!"

"We are all here to think the deepest thoughts of tree life and truth. And I am here to guide each of you into your future, happy tree life. And so I will say it again, that is why we are all here now in this place below this great mountain, on this foggy, sad morning, listening to deep truths of tree life, given by your favorite teacher, Thinking Teacher. Is that not right?"

All shouted, "Yes!!!"

"Say to the trees near you, 'I want the deepest truths of tree life.'"

Teacher waited a moment until the tree mumbling quieted down.

"In fact, speaking of truth, today, I have some very good news for you... But first, the bad news!"

All the trees of Think Orchard were getting very excited by now about all this news. It did sound very important. And each tree tried very hard not to think, or at least, not to think too loudly. There were more than a hundred trees in this orchard, after all. How could any-tree even hear Teacher if some of these trees happened to think a little too loudly? All were silent now.

"Thinkers, I have an important message from your Maker. It is so very important. Remember, I have been warning each of you daily that danger was coming, great pain and tree death, even all of our deaths! All of you are now very informed of the great dangers very near to each of you, here... now... on this hazy, frightful morning..."

below this great, threatening mountain... under this gray, watchful sky... Is that not right?!"

"Yes, Teacher!!!"

"In fact, we thinking trees now know that each of us will die a very painful death, and very soon! Even now!!!"

Now all the thinking trees were thinking quite loudly with very loud gasps.

"GGGaaassspppp!!!"

"Unless there is a real answer and soon, unless we can get some real help, we are all doomed! Think about that!!! So now, the message from your Maker! The message we thinking trees can all trust! Are you thinking trees ready for truth?!"

"Yes!!!"

"There! That tree over there! It calls itself Homer! Yesterday, it brought such great, painful death to our orchard! That evil tree brought our deaths!"

Now, there were great rumblings of deep thoughts, and the seeing knots of all were pointed right at me.

"Listen, Thinkers! No! Do not destroy that tree just yet! It is too late anyway! He has poisoned us all! Death will soon be upon each of us! No! Leave that poisonous, deadly tree alone for now! We must now think deeply on what we must do to be saved! We want to live our precious tree lives and not die!!! Not today!!!"

Oh, the great rumblings and the angry stares.

"Tell the trees near you, 'I don't want to die!!!'"

Again, there was much rumbling of mumblings, such sad and angry mumblings.

"Now, let each thinking tree think about how each tree feels. Listen carefully, now. All trees that feel very well and very healthy, raise your crowns up high! Now!!!"

All we thinkers raised our green crowns up high, Teacher raising his green and orange one.

"Oh!!! It's much worse than any-tree could ever think, much worse than even the Maker had thought! Sadly, feeling very well and healthy is a sure sign that death is near, even at your branches!

Oh, no!!! Clearly, we thinking trees are all in great danger of our tree lives!!! Feeling very well certainly means a quick, certain death!!!"

Oh, the misery and the anger I could see in these thinker trees, these trees who were trying so very hard not to think too loudly. Oh, if tree stares could kill, I would have already died a hundred deaths.

Teacher continued, "Do we thinking trees need more proof of the danger?! Of course not! We can all see the great danger we are in! But still... there is more proof! Every tree! How many of you... Be honest now! How many of you thinking trees heard this evil homer-tree shout with pain yesterday?! Raise your branches! Now!!!"

They all raised their branches up high, including Teacher and I. And all seeing knots were again set on me, set with the greatest anger.

"Oh, I can explain that..." I began to say. "You see, Teacher..."

"Silence, bad, bad tree!" shouted a guard as he struck my speech opening.

"Thank you, guards!" shouted Teacher. "You see, deepest thinker trees, that bad tree brought our enemy's poison here to our healthy, thinking orchard! Every-tree heard his great pain of nearing death, which he secretly carried into our orchard yesterday! Is that not right?!"

They all tried to say "Yes!" but it came out more like "YEGggrrriii!!!"

I had never heard a sound like that coming from a tree.

"He carried the great, hidden death here in his own evil trunk of death!!!"

Teacher turned to me and shouted, "Evil tree of death!!! Why did you come to our wonderful Think Orchard?!!!"

"GGGaaassspppp!!! GGGrrriii!!!"

He continued, "That bad tree brought pain and death here to destroy we-thinker-trees! Death is near! Near, I sssay! Ssso near!!! It'sss danger to usss all!!!"

All trees were shaking with great fear now, but one great thinker among all these thinkers then raised a branch to ask Teacher a question.

"Yes, you with the raised branch! Do you have a question?"

"Yeah, Teacher. Can we-thinker-trees do anything to live? What's the good news?"

"Very good question! That should be every thinking tree's question: 'What do we do now to live?! How can we live on without facing a sure and sudden painful loss of tree life, of all our tree lives?! Oh! The pain we all fear!!! What's the good news?!!!' Thank you for asking, Great Thinker!"

Teacher turned to every tree: "Are you all thinking?!"

"Yes!!!"

"Then tell a thinking tree next to you, "I'm thinking now! What about you?!"

Again, there was that great tree mumbling, all seeing knots pointed toward Teacher. And the two guards were holding me so tightly that I thought for sure that I would lose several branches very soon.

"Yes, the very bad news from your Maker also comes with some very good news! Life!!! You can keep your life! And since all we trees are deathly sick, which we know because we all feel so very well, we must hurry to save your... to save our-tree-selves!!!

The most dangerous of unseen, unfelt poisons must be removed with the very best help possible! And there is only one cure for this hidden, deadly poison! Your Maker is sending special help! Even now, his fiery, flying tree is on its way! Its healing fire is your only hope! Thinker trees, save your-tree-selves!!! Receive your Maker's flying tree of fire!!!"

"Flying tree of fire!!!" cried the thoughts of all thinkers.

Then Teacher said, "Let's call your Maker... With every crown bowed, 'Oh, Maker of trees and, I'm sure, lots of other things! We don't want to die! Not now! Not like this! Your tree of fire comes with healing in its flames! Oh, Maker! Bring it now!!! Abloom!'"

And all thinkers except me-tree said, "Abloom!"

I quietly asked the guards, "If you feel very well, isn't that a good thing?"

"Silence, poison tree! We heard your pain yesterday! You brought tree deaths!"

And then it appeared, the flying tree of flames! I had never seen such a thing, never even heard of one. Yes, it was a special tree, a flying fiery tree! But it looked like several trees. In fact, it looked like something was hiding inside of three or four walking trees. Were they tied around it, its flapping wings sticking out the sides? That's what it looked like to me as it circled about us.

I thought to my-tree-self, "Isn't that a crawler's tail hanging from the roots of those poor trees?"

A few trees heard my thoughts and mocked, "Ha! He sees a crawler's tail! Ha, ha, ha!"

Teacher looked our way: "Silence, stupid trees!" Then he looked about and shouted, "Every tree that wants to live another day, to the orchard center now!!!"

Then every tree, filled with panic, was pushing its way towards the middle of Think Orchard. But Teacher was now standing near its edge. And my guards had just left me and were quickly getting out of the orchard.

"Now's my chance!" I thought.

Here it came, flying straight toward Think Orchard, that flying crawler of flames hiding among those walking trees, those poor trees waving toward us! It was now so near, spitting out bright red flames, the heat warming my bark!

With the guards pushing their way through the orchard, I quickly got behind them, the three of us now running toward Teacher. But suddenly, that fiery flyer saw me running toward the edge of the orchard. It looked my way!

By now, every tree was crowding the orchard center, calling out to those poor trees above, "Me-tree! Me-tree! Save me-tree!!!"

I thought, "They don't understand. They're calling for their deaths."

But now, the swooshing wings and frying flames were flying right toward me! I shouted at my-tree-self, "Do something!" Then looking up beyond the sky, I cried out, "Help!!!"

At that very moment, as hot flames were stretching out to meet me, I saw another flying something I had never seen before. It looked like a woodsman, having the two walking roots and the two waving branches. But it had something more, very different from a woodsman! It had the two great wings of a sky-king! (Later, I was told this was an angel.)

It had flown in so very quickly and was right there above me, now sitting in the air between me and those very poor trees, the ones taken through the air by the fiery crawler! I felt some heat of the flames and saw their bright red all about me, but my friend with sky-king wings had covered me, blocking those killer flames.

And those flames must have bounced right off the angel; for Teacher got hit really hard by those same hot flames! Now, I could see that Teacher was burning, his tree crown now gone. What a surprise! An ugly, creepy-crawly head was sticking out instead!

And that smoking head was now shouting at the fiery crawler circling above, "You idiot! You stupid dragon! Don't fry me!!! Fry that tree!!! And then the orchard!!!"

You see, that smoking crawly head sticking out from the tree trunk was pointing at me! And so the flying dragon circled back around and shot its red flames again, straight at me, with the angel again blocking them. And again, those frying flames were redirected toward the fake-tree teacher.

By now, it looked like a dead, well-fried dragon head, hanging down the side of a burning, smoking tree trunk. Though it was swinging about from side to side like the waves of great waters, it was surely dead. Dark red flames were now bursting out from that broken dragon head, carrying with them great sounds of "Pop! Pop!! Pop!!!" and "Kaaapluey!!!"

While its sizzling head was still waving about, I turned and saw the guards racing away in a hurry.

"I've got to see where they go and who they meet." I thought.

I raced after them. They were very fast for walking trees. They must have been fakes too. But surprisingly, I was faster than them.

I thought, "I'm so fast! I lost all but my head, but I gained so much more!"

I caught up with them and hid behind a large rock. I could see who was waiting for them. It was my friend Truly and... Stanamon! Oh, how surprised I was!

The two guards quickly ran up to them and fell before Stanamon. They shouted, "King!!! Dragon teacher is dead!!!"

"How could this happen?! Report!!!"

"King, all trees were ready for frying, and the dragon came flying, but there was another tree there, a homer tree!!!"

"Yes? Speak!!!"

"The dragon spit flames at the homer tree, but an angel covered it, and the flames turned toward dragon teacher! Dragon teacher burned! King, he's fried!!!"

"What?!!! How could this be?!!!"

Then Stanamon turned to Truly: "It was your simple job to destroy that tree! Why did this happen?!!!"

Truly said, "King! Dragon teacher told me he could handle it! The flying dragon was going to fry that tree!!!"

"Silence!!!"

Stanamon turned toward the two guards and shouted, "You two! Return to the castle now and report for kitchen duty!!!"

"Yes, King!!!"

As the two guards turned toward the castle, one turned back toward Stanamon and said, "But King! I don't know how to cook!"

Stanamon answered, "Hogchef will teach you! To the kitchen now!!!"

The two guards left, and now Stanamon turned back to Truly: "You Fool! You failed your simple task! Now find that stupid tree and finish your job!"

"Yes, King!!!"

"Oh, if you fail again, you also will have kitchen duty!"

"Yes, King!!!"

Truly was turning, but Stanamon added,

"I'm sure you'll make a fine dessert!"

"Yes, King! I will not fail!!!"

8

CLOUDS OF BRAMBLE

I turned and quickly raced back to Think Orchard. I told my-tree-self, "Oh, how quick you are now with this super trunk from the Maker!"

I got back to Think Orchard and thought, "Will they kill me?"

But with their fake-tree teacher now dead and his power over their thinking gone, the thinking trees seemed to wake as if from a dream.

"What happened? Where's Teacher?" thought each thinking tree.

"That, thinking trees, was your teacher, that frying earth-crawler hiding in a tree! That was Teacher!"

"What?! How could this be? That was Teacher?!"

"Yes! Your tree elder was a lying creepy-crawly! Did you see his guards quickly running away?!"

They all nodded "Yes!"

"See! They too were fakes! And they ran!"

"But what of our first teacher? Did the creepy-crawly kill him?"

"It must have."

"And the deadly, hidden poison? Was that fake too?"

"Now, you are thinking trees. Yes, of course! Feeling well and healthy is a good thing!"

"But what about the fiery, healing tree of the skies?"

We trees looked out and saw the flying dragon that fried the tree dragon. It was flying about in the distance.

I said, "It's a flying earth-crawler that spits fire. It's carrying some poor walking trees tied around it!"

"GGGAAASSSPPP!!!"

"That burning earth-crawly in the tree called that one flying over there a dragon. And it looks like your teacher was a dragon too! Now do you know who the bad tree really was?"

"Oh sorry, Homer. Our teacher was the bad one. We weren't thinking."

"No, you trees weren't thinking. The dragon in that tree tricked your minds using several tricks! Now, listen, and I'll tell you something interesting. It's what I told your dragon teacher yesterday."

When every tree had calmed down, stopped thinking so loudly, and was ready to listen to more, I told them a little of my third dream.

And then all at once, thinking-tree thoughts brightened each tree, and they all spoke out, "Teacher was the dragon in your dream!!!"

"Yes," I said. "And it was the enemy of all trees and of everything good! It was the enemy of our Maker! Thinking trees, don't listen to an earth-crawly in a tree! That flying fiery dragon over there wasn't sent by our Maker! Don't believe anything a dragon says!"

"Yeah! Tree dragon is dead!!!"

"Yes," I thought. "Now, we trees can do some real thinking about tree life!"

And then I remembered our helper. "Oh! Where's our help, the two-rooter with sky-king wings?!"

We trees looked around and then up, and there he was. He was still there, sitting in the sky above us. That must have been why the frying dragon was circling in the distance.

We trees all shouted up to him, "Thank you!"

And with a smile he replied, "Why thank me? Thank our Maker! For he sent me! Farewell, Freed Orchard!"

"Farewell!!!" we all shouted.

And then I called out, up past the sky, "Thank you, our Maker!"

And all freed thinking trees called out as well, "Thank you, Maker!!!"

I said, "Freed Orchard? Don't you like that more than Think Orchard?"

"Yes!" They all shouted. "We are Freed Orchard!!!"

"Well," I said. "The sun will be falling pretty soon. And tomorrow when the sun returns, I'll be walking home."

"Where's home?" asked one Freed-tree.

"Oh, home is with my family at Love Orchard. You Freed-trees are free to walk home together with me, if you like. But you don't have to, of course. Freed-trees are free to decide."

"Yes!!!" they all shouted without a moment to think.

Some continued, "Tomorrow, we'll walk home with you! Dragon teacher is dead, and we are free to leave this lonely place!"

Then they all together thought out loud, "Homer's home's home!!!"

"Very good," I said. "But I want to mention one important thing about home."

Some said, "What is it, Teacher?"

"Teacher? Hmmm... Well, Love Orchard is my home away from home. Our true home is up beyond the skies with our Maker. That's home forever. But for now, Love Orchard makes a very good home away from home."

I could see that only a few trees understood. So I added, "We can talk about this more later. But for tonight, let's think about how to walk home, and then we'll talk about it when the sun rises."

"Very good," they all said. "Good rest."

"Good rest, Freed Orchard," I said. But then I thought, "How will we trees get home? Which way is home?"

The next morning as sunlight was reaching over and around the great mountain, there was a buzzing sound.

"Oh, no!" I thought. "It's them!"

I looked up and there they were! The flying trunk and its two-rooter!

Feeling groggy, I shouted, "Every tree jump!"

"Where?!" they all asked.

"Anywhere!" I shouted, as I jumped and dropped to the earth. I could hear trees jumping and dropping. I looked up again.

The flying trunk was swinging from side to side, just like it did to my family before. And the two-rooter was waving a branch. "Oh, no! What danger will we trees face now?" I asked my-tree-self.

"No danger just yet," said a little voice. I looked behind me. It was the little bramble!

"No danger?" I said, still listening to that buzzing sound from above.

"No danger," said the bramble. "I'll explain about Woodbee and his friend, later."

"Woodbee and his friend? Do you mean that flying trunk and two-rooter up there?"

"Yes."

It then looked like the little bramble waved a branch or two toward those two flying above, the trunk still swinging about and the two-rooter still waving. Soon, but not soon enough, they were flying away into the distant sky.

I turned to the little bramble and asked, "Who are they?"

"Later, Friend. I'll explain later. Listen... Don't look behind you."

I took just a quick look and said, "Truly's coming this way."

"Homer, beware the traitor. Truly's no friend."

"I know."

Just then Truly walked up to us, and the little bramble said, "Here's your friend, Truly!"

Truly said to me, "You know what?"

I said, "Oh, nothing. Hi, Truly!"

"Hi, Homer."

Truly looked over at the bramble a moment and then took me aside. He whispered, "I need to talk to you... alone."

"Oh, okay."

I followed him some distance away, the little bramble carefully watching us, I think. You know, a bramble's face is a little hard to see.

Truly stopped and turned to me: "Homer! I'm so glad you're safe! I worried about you! That little bramble is dangerous!"

"Yes, I know, Truly. But I'm okay. Say, where did you go?"

"Just like I always do. Maybe you noticed... I've been watching out for you, Homer. When that dangerous, little bramble goes off somewhere, I follow him to see what he's up to."

"And what has he been up to?"

"Just like before, Homer, he's been talking with our enemies. Last time it was an ugly creepy-crawly, but this time he talked with some creepy, old two-rooter, who wore all black and had an ugly gray face."

"Oh, I've seen him!"

"You have?"

"Yes, that sounds like Stanamon. He kept sending out hungry-runners after me."

"Really? Stanamon? Well, stay away from the dangerous, little bramble, Homer."

"Okay. I'll try, Friend. Thank you."

"What are friends for?"

I'm sure Truly didn't like it, but I walked back to Freed Orchard, walking right up to the little bramble. Truly followed along some but kept his distance. He stayed over at the edge of the orchard.

I said, "Little bramble! Say, where have you been?"

"I've been away to Brambleland."

"And why Brambleland?"

"I called out the Bramble Force. Look out there and you'll see."

I looked about with great surprise! There were thousands upon thousands of brambles, as far as the seeing knot could see!

"Oh! So many brambles! Where did they all come from? And why are they here?! Do you come in peace?!"

"Oh, that depends... peace to you, Friend, but to any fire-breathing dragon, we offer no peace."

"Oh, I see... Fire-breathing dragon... You mean like the fiery thing in the sky that was flying around while hidden in some trees yesterday?"

"Yes, like that one."

"It came to destroy us, but a great winged two-rooter stopped its flames, bouncing them from me toward the earth-crawler teacher inside the tree."

"Yes, I know. And that lying snake is now dead."

"Lying snake? I keep learning new words lately. But how do you know, little bramble, about the... the lying snake... and the flying dragon? Were you here? I didn't see you."

"No, I wasn't here. But our Maker showed me what was happening, and so I know."

"Our Maker? You know Him?"

"Yes, of course. He sent me to help you, from the very beginning when we first met on the mountain."

"He did?"

"Yes. That's why I kept disappearing. I was watching Truly when he left us. I needed to see where he went, who he talked to."

"And who did Truly talk to?"

"Sometimes a snake. But this last time, he met with Stanamon."

"I see..."

The little bramble continued, "But there's still more to do. We must get you and your tree friends to Love Orchard safely and quickly."

"You know about Love Orchard? Oh, little bramble, who are you?"

"I'll explain later, but for now, we must be on our way."

"Can I trust this little bramble?" I quietly thought to myself. "After all, my friend Truly, turned out to be my enemy. Can I trust this little bramble?"

"Yes, you can," said the little bramble.

"Oh, you heard my thoughts?"

"Hard not to. But why ask your-tree-self? Why not ask our Maker? Ask Him. I'll wait."

I had a moment. Truly was still standing out at the edge of the orchard. So I turned and walked away from the little bramble for a bit and looked up past the cloudy sky and said, "Oh, Maker of trees and all things, and I suppose even brambles, oh, my Maker, what am I to do? Should I trust this little bramble? Should I go with him and his army of brambles?"

After a moment, the bramble asked, "And?"

"Well, this is new for me... I hadn't thought of asking for things like this, but yes, it does seem that I can trust you, little bramble."

"Well, good! Let's be off then!"

"Off? Oh, what does that mean?"

"Homer, gather together all your friends! Everyone must be ready to leave very soon! The rest, I will show you!"

"Oh, what could this mean?" I wondered. And then I asked the little bramble, "Truly, too?"

"Truly, too. Don't worry. I've got it under control with our Maker's help. Invite Truly to join us."

So I went about announcing to all the Freed-trees and to Truly, "Every-tree! We're going to my home away from home! We're leaving for Love Orchard! Every-tree, be ready very soon! We're traveling with the bramble army!"

Truly quickly walked up to me and said, "What are you doing? You can't go with that bramble! You'll be in great danger! You know that! Don't go!"

"Truly, I have to go with him. What else can I do? I don't know where I am or how to get back home. Don't worry. If there's any danger, I'll be ready to escape. Truly, you can join us if you like."

Now Truly looked truly worried, even scared. He just stood there looking at me for a bit, quietly thinking, so quietly that I couldn't hear a word. Finally, he said, "Homer, can't I talk you out of going with this bramble army?"

"Sorry, Truly, you can't. I have to go. You know, 'Home's the place...'."

"What? Home's the place? Well... okay. But I'll go with you. Be ready to escape if there's any danger. I'll watch out for you, Friend."

"Okay..."

I had told all the trees to be ready to leave very soon, but, of course, every tree was ready immediately. We trees don't need anything but the sun, rain, and earth. We've all been ready to go since our seedling days. But the little bramble had not yet explained to me how we were going.

"Little bramble! We trees are ready to go! And Truly's coming, too."

"Good!" he said.

He then looked out at his vast bramble army before us and shouted like only a bramble general could, "Bramble Force! For our Maker! Cloud formation! Now!!!"

We trees were caught by surprise, and that almost never happens. All those many thousands of brambles now began to come together, one by one and then ten by ten and soon hundred by hundred, into something very much like a giant cloud! But no! I looked again. There were many clouds of bramble!

"What can this mean?" I thought.

"You shall see, my friend," said the little bramble.

And see I did! There were by now around a hundred giant green and brown bramble clouds before us, resting on the earth!

Then all these great bramble clouds burst out in song!

"Bramble Force! Ready to take wing!

For our Maker and our king!"

I asked the little bramble, "King? Are you their king?"

"We'll talk later, my friend! Up we go then! Homer, have two trees together mount one bramble cloud! Each tree can help the other! Here! This one is yours and Truly's! It's next to mine!"

I turned and shouted to Freed Orchard, "Brother trees, two trees together on one cloud! Help each other! And be safe! We'll be off soon!!! Truly! You and I can share this cloud!"

"Okay..." said Truly, looking worried.

And I thought, "Will we roll, or will we fly? Will we go the right way? Will we ever get home?"

"Don't worry! You will see, my friend!"

Trees mounted their clouds in pairs, with Truly and I sitting on one cloud, the little bramble sitting alone on his.

Then the little bramble shouted out his orders, "Bramble Force! For our Maker! Take wing!"

"What?! What are we doing?!" I was surprised by our cloud's jump upward! And now all clouds were jumping up toward the sky!

In no time at all, bramble clouds were lifting up toward the cloudy sky, each carrying two walking trees. But, of course, one cloud carried a lone, little bramble.

I shouted to the bramble, "But how will your brambles ever break free from each other?!"

"Oh, you worry too much! You will see when that time comes!"

We were quickly rising higher into the sky. And I began to wonder, "Why the hurry?"

Then our Maker sent a strong wind, which quickly carried our forest of clouds away from that lonely place, the sun still rising behind us.

Oh! The beauty of that morning! The high sky was of blue, clouds below of white, and even further below, forests of green. And we trees and a little bramble were up here between hills and sky, riding greenish brown clouds of bramble!

Our bramble clouds were leaving Sunrise Mountain far behind us. There were hills and great waters as far as one could see to the left. And to the right, there were only hazy flat lands.

But soon after, there was rising gray smoke, looking like the gray trunks of huge trees, along those flat lands to the right.

As I looked closer, I could see bright red flames shooting up and out from the earth, hundreds of them! It looked as though an angry earth was spitting out trees of fire, their smoke rising up into the skies.

"How curious." I thought. "What could possibly be growing these flaming trees, these fiery trees sprouting up from the earth? Is there any danger to us on our clouds?"

The little bramble shouted out to me, "Don't worry! It's alright! I'll explain later!"

My fiery-forest question had to be left unanswered for now. And so I thought, "It's still such a wonderful morning! The little bramble must be right about all those trees of fire below. They really are far below us. Besides, what could possibly go wrong way up here on clouds of bramble, way up here in this beautiful sky?"

Truly. Truly was sitting near me on our cloud, but still, he got even closer. Suddenly, Truly got right next to me and shouted, "Look down there! Is that a dragon?!"

I tightly held on to our bramble cloud as Truly bumped into me. He was acting like he was trying to watch a dragon.

I said, "A dragon?!"

Truly's plan became clear, but before he could push me over the edge, the little bramble shouted out orders to our cloud, "Truly gone!!! Now!!!"

Suddenly, our cloud opened up just below Truly! Where there was once cloud, there was now only the earth far below! So Truly quickly slipped past me, trying his best to grab something, anything, including me! But I was firmly holding onto our cloud by then!

So he just slipped away, dropping toward the empty sky and earth below! I could hear him getting torn some by the bramble stickers on his way down! And I heard his cries for help, "Help!!! Help me!!!" for some time.

He was shouting and yelling all the way down. But down he kept dropping and dropping, like a rock. And I kept watching and watching to see what would happen to my friend Truly.

When he finally reached the end, fortunately for Truly, he dropped right into great waters with a great splash. As we trees quickly flew along on our clouds, I could barely see the splashing. Truly's roots and crown were still splashing about.

I thought, "Well, Truly, my friend who was no friend, is still alive." And I wondered, "Will he return to Stanamon? Is he that foolish?"

The little bramble answered, "He truly is foolish! He became our Maker's enemy! And, yes, he was no friend! I wondered how long before you'd learn that! But better late than never!"

Earlier, when we had lifted off on our clouds, I had asked my-tree-self, "Why the hurry?" Now, I did not have to wonder. Just as Truly splashed into the waters below, I saw it. And I shouted, "Bramble! Look! A dragon!!!"

The fiery dragon was heading straight for the little bramble and I, spitting out red flames at some unfortunate trees and bramble clouds along the way, as it swung its fiery head back and forth. A few bramble clouds suddenly burst into flames, the fires disappearing some poor clouds of bramble. I saw some trees moving about, some jumping off their clouds toward others below them! And trees were moving around, making some space on their clouds for others!

"Oh! What will become of us, we trees and bramble friends!"

The little bramble shouted, "You shall see!"

And with that, as the fire-breathing dragon came near to me and the bramble, I saw what a little bramble can do. He ran to the edge of his cloud, set himself down low on his roots, and with a shout, the little bramble sprang out in a jump I had never seen before!

He shouted, "Dragon, die this day! For our Maker!!!"

And with that shout, the little bramble dropped like a sky-king does when aiming for a hungry-runner, dropping straight through red flames into the dragon's fiery opening.

I shouted, "Stickler! My friend! My true friend!!!"

Stickler was gone! And the dragon was now looking about wildly, its eyes bulging, looking first at me and then at clouds of bramble! Its red seeing knots opened wider and wider till red and purple flames burst out from its trunk! The dragon was then spinning round and round, wing following wing, falling, falling like a ripe fruit from a giant tree, flaming red and purple all the while.

"Stickler, my friend! 'Stickler!!!'"

I couldn't watch the falling fiery dragon to its end. Something was in my seeing knots.

And bramble clouds began to rain, raining tears for a king. I shouted for them to stop the clouds and help Stickler, but they pointed out that other dragons were coming from a distance, coming our way.

And the brambles of my cloud answered me, "Our king gave us orders! We must get you and your friends home! This we must do! Besides, we don't know how to stop!!!"

That was that. Our stormy clouds of bramble continued flying on great winds for home, bramble rains falling along the way. For some time then, I could see little of what lay before or behind. Heavy rains of brambles were clouding my sight. Also, my own seeing knots were no help. You see, I sprouted my own rain clouds.

"Oh, Stickler! I will never forget!" I wondered, "Why did I lose my best friend?!"

Don't ask me why. But even then, even after all that my little friend went through for us, I still waited for his answer. After all, he always had an answer for me, even if it was, "I'll explain later!" But, no, there was no answer. There was only the hushed howling of winds and rain.

9

A TREE'S TALE ENDS

On that same day, we trees of bramble clouds reached home. I could see every tree standing before us, ready to welcome us home! I shouted to every bramble cloud, "There! That's Love Orchard!" And I added for the Bramble-cloud trees, "We're home!"

Later, family and friends told me what they thought when we trees arrived on clouds of bramble. Some-tree had looked out and shouted, "Look! Dark storm clouds coming our way! Every-tree, take cover!"

Oh, the surprise of all in Love Orchard when they saw that we were trees on friendly clouds of bramble. Oh, so happy we all were! There were shouts of joy when my family and I saw each other after those many moons!

"Eve! Ray!"

"Homer!"

"Dad!"

Family and friends welcomed me, Freed Orchard, and our bramble friends of the clouds. This was now Freed Orchard's new home. And I... I was finally home. I gave both Eve and Ray a big tree hug.

Then Ray said, "Dad, every good tale begins with a seed."

"Yes," I said. "But where did that come from? Is another good tale beginning?"

"Here," Ray said. "Dad, meet Sunshine, my wife! Sunshine, this is my dad!"

"Sunshine is your wife?! Oh, that's wonderful! Hi Sunshine! Glad to meet you!"

"And me-tree also! I've heard a lot about you! May I call you, 'Dad'?"

"'Dad'? Yes, of course! Now, where is this seed of a good tale Ray spoke of?"

"She's a seedling now, Dad! And her name's Windy! Come on, Dad! We'll introduce you!" And then Ray added, "Oh... welcome home, Dad!"

"Welcome home, Dad!" said Sunshine.

"Yes! Welcome home, Homer!"

My happy family and I then began to walk over to see the little seedling, but no, I couldn't hold my adventures to my-tree-self much longer.

"Family, do you want to hear about one adventure?"

"Yes, we trees do!" they shouted.

"And I can't wait to tell you! Oh! The adventures I've walked through with our Maker's help! Oh! Stanamon, Great Sky-king, the woodsmen, my tree head rolling all about, huge water-flyers, a friendly traitor, and oh, the dragons! And, oh, I will never forget my best friend Stickler, the little bramble king! And, oh! There were the flames, clouds of bramble, and such dangers! Oh! So many adventures to tell!"

"But," Eve added. "Please, Homer, no more dreams!"

"Yes, Eve! Ha, ha, ha! No more dreams! And let's hope no more flying trunk with two-rooter, too!"

"Dad, tree-flyer!"

"Oh, yes, Ray, that's right. Tree-flyer."

"No, Dad! I mean, 'Look up there! It's Tree-flyer!'"

Yes, I now heard it. And then I looked up.

"Bzzzzzzz!!!"

And, yes, they were doing that swinging and waving thing again, which always means trouble.

"Every-tree, jump!"

But thankfully, they were just passing by. And the buzzing soon faded.

"Here, Dad! Let me give you a branch!"

Ray helped me get back up on my roots.

"Thanks, Son! Say, Sunshine! Where's that little Windy Seedling of yours! Come on, Eve, let's go before Swoopertrunk comes back!"

"Homer!"

"Dad, it's Tree-flyer!"

"Oh, yeah... that's right." And then I just had to stop and say, "Family, Home's the place..."

"you'd never leave..." continued Eve.

"even if you..." said Ray.

"ever could," added Sunshine.

"And this tree could and did... but finally flew back home on clouds of bramble! Come on, Family. First, I'll tell you about Great Sky-king!"

Now for one reason or another (may the reader understand), a season has passed since we flew those clouds of bramble home. And just recently, my little crown-flyer friend, Sky-Ranger, brought me some news; for she is always very busy with her favorite hobby, spying. That's what sky-rangers do, after all, when they have the time. So I gladly received her report, which I have included in my final comments below:

As this brief tree's tale begins to end, I can
inform you that Grandad is busy preparing another
surprise "Welcome Home" party for me, while I, of
course, prepare for my surprise visit.

What of the seven orchards, Loveless, Rich,
Castle, Stone, Death, Love, and Poor? Well, some in
Stone Orchard still please our Maker, while
Jezeltree trains students of darkness in the evil
which some in Castle Orchard have learned on
their own from their ancient writings. Loveless
Orchard still stands for truth while falling short of
love, but Love Orchard still lives for the love of
their Maker.

What of the three remaining orchards that
couldn't see what their Maker sees? Well, many at
Rich Orchard still feel poor while living rich; most
at Poor Orchard still feel rich while living miserably
poor; and most at Death Orchard still take pride in
living while dying.

What of evil? Well, Serp Forest is still
troubling those trees that follow their Maker;
Serpothel keeps messaging Stanamon about a
walking tree, while Stanamon keeps avoiding him

just a little bit longer; and Truly is still hiding under a pile of rocks far away from a gray worm's castle, while Stanamon's beast-men search for him everywhere.

What of my new friends? Well, Freed Orchard calls Love Orchard their home away from home; Jill, the friendly two-rooter, is writing her adventure story called *Shipwreck on Homer's Island* (I need to find someone who knows what 'shipwreck' and 'island' mean.), while her parents watch with concern; half the Bramble Force is still trying to free themselves, while the other half is keeping the Love Orchard skies dragon-free; and Great Sky-king occasionally visits Love Orchard, where He offers helpful suggestions to a promising tree author, who is now very close to completing his first book of adventures, *The Great Adventures of a Common Walking Tree*.

Well again, for one reason or another (may the reader understand, and I know tree readers will), several seasons have passed since my return home on clouds of bramble.

And it was on this beautiful, sunny morning that I saw something wonderful in our clearing! A twister of colors! Yes, it was a low twisting cloud of flying flowers! I had never seen anything like this! I asked myself, "A new beginning? But how odd! It's a twister of flowers, not of clouds in the sky at all! Now what kind of new season could this be?" I wondered aloud.

Now I must mention that, of course, this tree's tale still must end as it started, as they always do, with a little seed, which by now is that sweet sapling, our very own little Windy. You see, Windy came by to watch me write, again.

"Meee-treee walky-walky!"

"Ray! Sunshine! Please get your little sapling! She's walking all through my adventure notes... again!"

"Homer!"

"Honey, you know how long it's taken me to get my first adventure book this far, with our dear, little Windy always getting into everything! I can't find anything anymore!"

"Homer!"

"Yes, Dear?!"

"We have visitors!"

"Who, Eve?!"

She pointed a branch at a little bramble:
"Look! Do you know him?!"

"What?!!! Stickler?! My friend?! I mean...
King Stickler?! But how...?!"

"Homer! Good to see you, Friend! It's always
Stickler to you!"

"Great to see you! I don't understand, but
I'm happy, of course! How did you escape from the
belly of a fiery dragon?! I mean how did you live
through that?! You did live through that, didn't
you?! You're not a ghost, are you?!!!"

"Friend, that's a lot of questions for a little
bramble after a very long journey, but I can say
this, 'I thank our Maker that He helps even us little
brambles!' Besides that? Well, Homer... I'll explain
later!

Oh! Let me introduce you! Homer and Eve!
This is Thorncesca, Queen of Brambleland, my
wife! Thorncesca, this is Homer and his wife Eve!"

"Oh, pleased to meet you both! I've heard so much about you, Homer!"

Eve said, "Oh, pleased to meet you both, too!"

King of Brambleland said, "So nice to finally meet you, Eve!"

And I said, "So nice to meet you, Queen of Brambleland! I'm so privileged to have your husband, the king, as a friend!"

King of Brambleland then said, "Hey! Let's take a walk, my friend! We've got another adventure from our Maker, if you're interested. Homer... this one may be dangerous."

"Friend, my middle name is 'Danger'."

"Really? What's your last name, Homer?"

"HELP!!!"

"Ha, ha, ha!"

"Ha, ha, ha! You know, Stickler, since you disappeared into that dragon and we all arrived here at Love Orchard, I've already had a few more adventures, including a battle both my son and I joined. We fought alongside my friend, the Ruler of Woodbee Island."

"Yes, I know."

"You do? You're kidding! How could you know about that? Stickler, you can't know everything!"

"Yes, my friend, I know that too."

"Ha, ha, ha! Well... I almost have enough adventures for a second book after I finish this first one!"

"Well, then maybe you're ready for another adventure!"

"Homer?"

"Eve, we'll be back soon. We're just going out for a short walk. We've got some bramble and tree things to talk about."

"Okay... You two take your walk. Queen of Brambleland and I have some things to discuss, too."

"That's right, Eve. And, oh, please call me 'Thorncesca'."

"Oh, okay, Thorncesca. Oh, Homer! You know, you have to finish your adventure book before going off on any new adventures!"

"Yes, Dear!"

Stickler asked, "So, Homer, when will you be done with this first adventure book you're working on?"

"Stickler, my friend... it's done!"

"Ha, ha, ha! You're the funniest walking tree I know!"

"Stickler, how many walking trees do you know?"

"Only you, my friend."

"Ha, ha, ha! Now, what were you saying about another adventure?"

"Wait, my friend. I'll explain soon... Oh! What's that?! What's that buzzing sound?!"

"What?! It's that flying trunk?! Again?! What now?!"

And yes, I quickly dropped to the ground, just to be on the safe side.

"Ha, ha! Homer, I was only joking!"

"Only joking? Joking about that flying trunk that swooped down on my family and made us jump off a cliff?! Only joking?"

"Yes, Homer. Woodbee saved your family's life, you know."

"Well, yes, I guess. But I wasn't sure... Like, why is he always buzzing around when something big is beginning or ending or when there's great danger? Stickler, can you tell me that?"

"Good questions, my friend. Yes, we'll start with Woodbee, and then we'll talk about our next adventure. Okay?"

"Oh, okay..."

"You see, Homer, Woodbee often comes flying around for a reason, for a very good reason."

"Really?"

"Really. But don't take my word for it. Come on! I'll let his human friend explain it all to you!"

"What?! When?!"

"Now."

"Can't we just go on that next great adventure first?!"

"Ha, ha, ha! What do you think, my friend?"

"Maybe?"

"Oh, Homer... Do you know whose sapling that is walking over there?"

"Sapling? Walking? Stickler, where are you pointing? Which direction?"

"Oh... over there!"

"There? Oh, no! Is that Windy? Windy! Come back! Stickler, I'll be right back!"

"Ha, ha! I'll believe it when I see it!"

"Windy, don't walk that way! No, Windy! Stop! Ray! Sunshine!"

"Bzzzzzzzzzzzzzz!"

"Meee-treee! Walky-walky!"

"Oh, no! Oh, my Maker! Help!!!"

ABOUT THE AUTHOR

*John Evans was first drawn to the great outdoors
in California, where he grew up. As a kid, he
would explore hundred-year-old goldmine camps
in the Sierra Nevada mountains, catching water
bugs, tree frogs, river turtles, alligator lizards,
king snakes, and mountain scorpions along the
way. He and his friends would often ride their
stingrays out to the San Joaquin River for long
summer weekends of camping, swimming, and
fishing.*

*Later in life, he explored alleys, hills,
valleys, and islands in Korea and China. He
taught English as a second language (ESL) for
more than thirty years in the USA, Korea, and
China. For he has a graduate degree in linguistics.
He and his wife now live in South Korea, with
occasional visits to Texas, Mongolia, and Nepal.*

*After reading book one, The Great
Adventures of a Common Walking Tree, in this
series, Woodbee Island Tales, check out book two,
The Ruler of Woodbee Island. Also, watch for*

future books in his series. And you can visit one of his six blogs at

https://johnnysblogcabin.wordpress.com/

ABOUT THE ILLUSTRATOR

Cynthia Jackson is an accomplished graphic artist and illustrator with a unique artistic talent. She has been doing artwork professionally for more than twenty-five years.

Cynthia has illustrated for various organizations. She has done years of computer graphics for building programs and adult education. She has also contributed to children-education curriculums, which include crafts, bulletin-board designs, children vacation-school art, murals, graphic designs, and more.

It is evident through her artwork that Cynthia has an enduring passion for a fulfilled life, both for her and for others, which can clearly be seen in her art.

One such proof for this passion in life is her published coloring journal, "Journal of an Insane Woman," which guides the reader-turned-illustrator through some difficult thoughts and emotions in order to find peace in life. Cynthia's creative art captures the beholder's imagination for their benefit.

Also, Cynthia did the wonderful illustrations for book 2 of this series, The Ruler of Woodbee Island. Enjoy more of Cynthia's artwork at her website, which has free downloadable coloring sheets: Free Printable Coloring Pages - Life Changing Art (cindyworldart.com)

TRUE HAPPILY EVER AFTER

It's been said, "Life after 'Happily Ever After' has its surprises, struggles, betrayals, battles, and, of course, bouts with dragons." This is true for each of us while in this world, even if only spiritually sometimes. There is no "Happily Ever After" here in this world.

Why? Because this world wasn't made for that. Our hero in his Woodbee Island world cried out to his Maker, and his Maker helped him. Our real world is where we, too, call out to our Maker, receiving His help.

Who is our Maker? He is the Creator of the heavens and the earth. He is the only God. He sent His only Son into the world to be born a baby. And this human baby named Jesus, who was, is, and always will be God, grew up in our world. Jesus lived, taught, did many miracles, and then died a horrific death for our sins on a cross in the land of Israel in the Middle East. But... after three days, God raised Him from the dead! He lives! Jesus then returned to heaven, where He is now waiting for that right time to return to earth, but this time He will be both King and Judge of all. And we have all done wrong and deserve death.

The good news? Jesus died for us, for all of us. If we believe in God's only Son Jesus Christ, all our sins are then gone forever. Then we have the real happily ever after, a wonderful forever with our God, who loves us. It's important to understand that the alternative to heaven with Jesus forever is a hell of flames and torment forever. You see, true happily ever after is found only in Jesus Christ.

LIFE-CHANGING NEWS:
First the BAD, and then the **GOOD**

... for all have sinned,
and fall short of the glory of God ...
Romans 3:23

For the wages of sin is death,
but the free gift of God is eternal life
in Christ Jesus our Lord.
Romans 6:23

But God commends his own love toward us,
in that while we were yet sinners,
Christ died for us.
Romans 5:8

For God so loved the world,
that he gave his one and only Son,
that whoever believes in him
should not perish,
but have eternal life.
John 3:16

... that if you will confess with your mouth
that Jesus is Lord,
and believe in your heart
that God raised him from the dead,
you will be saved.
Romans 10:9

(All scripture references are from the World English Bible.)

JESUS IS LORD!

Made in the USA
Las Vegas, NV
25 July 2023

75235504R00139